IN THE DARKNESS

A Project Artemis Novel

K.M. SCOTT

ANINA COLLINS

In The Darkness

Persephone Gilmore comes from a life of privilege. The oldest daughter of media mogul Marshall Gilmore, she grew up wanting for nothing. But her father taught her more than just how to make billions, and even though she could sit by the pool and eat bon bons every day for the rest of her life, she chooses to work as an ER nurse and live on her own away from the family estate and her father's security.

Then one night, those choices come back to haunt her.

Nick Hanson hasn't been truly happy since he left the FBI. Life as a hired gun for wealthy clients has paid well and made him very much in demand, but it isn't the same as the life he used to have. When Marshall Gilmore wants to hire him to rescue his daughter after she's taken hostage by a terrorist group, he agrees, but to save her, he'll have to go undercover and become one of them. It's dangerous work, but he knows what to expect and he's never been one to turn down a challenge.

What starts out as just another case turns into something much more, and Nick finds out just how much he's willing to do to save Persephone.

Chapter One

THE HEAVY SOUND of the metal elevator doors closing behind her made Persephone snap her head back to check that no one stood there. She'd ridden up to the second floor alone, so she had no reason to think anyone was behind her.

But still, she looked back.

Late nights never bothered her as much as the darkness that went along with them. Working until three in the morning didn't unnerve her, but walking to her car after her shift at the hospital always made her feel vulnerable, even if it meant she only had to walk across the bridge that connected the main building to the parking garage. She knew it was probably silly to worry since no one in the hospital's history had ever even been mugged going to their car. In fact, if it wasn't dark, she wouldn't have given it a second thought.

But it was dark.

In fact, as she hurried out of the bridge and onto level two of the garage, she wished she had taken her father up on his offer to have one of his security men escort her to and from her vehicle each night.

She quickly pushed that thought out of her mind with a silent scolding for him and herself. She wasn't a child anymore. Yes, she would always be his child—his oldest of three daughters—but she'd long passed the age when she needed anyone to guard her safety.

A twenty-eight year old woman didn't need some guy following her around all the time. Talk about cock blocking. Her father would have sent the biggest and meanest looking man he employed. Persephone knew him far too well. He would have made her have some Cro-Magnon guy tail her day and night. She had a feeling it would have been the fulfillment of every wish he'd had since she announced she planned to move away from the estate and live on her own.

Marshall Gilmore liked to say he had more money than God, who Persephone suspected had little use for one man's comparisons, even if he was the owner of seventeen television stations, six newspapers, and the most successful media conglomerate in the history of the world. And her father liked to throw that money around, especially when it came to getting his own way.

But Persephone hadn't succumbed to the almighty dollar and stood her ground when she decided she wanted to live on her own and have her own career. Her parents had hemmed and hawed over her choice like she had announced she planned to give up life on this planet for a stint on Mars, dangling all sorts of offers to tempt her into staying at their twenty-five acre estate. They'd build her a home of her own if she'd only stay. It would have a private entrance away from the main house. They'd release her trust fund money in a lump sum instead of having it come to her in parts as it already did.

They offered everything under the sun, and Persephone knew her father would have put the sun on the bargaining table if he had control of it to keep her living at the Gilmore estate. What they didn't understand was her choice wasn't about extracting more money from them. Just by being born a Gilmore meant she'd have more than enough money for anything she'd ever want to do in life.

She chose to move away to her own two-bedroom apartment, even though it didn't have acres of land surrounding it and even though she had not a single person to wait on her day and night there, because she wanted freedom.

The problem was at that very moment in the darkness of the Christie Medical Center parking garage that freedom she'd fought so hard for felt frighteningly lonely. And that made her feel vulnerable, something she'd hated feeling since she was a little girl.

Persephone quickly scanned level two of the garage and saw her silver BMW parked in the corner spot she tried to snag whenever she could. It meant her car had some light shining on it from the streetlight directly outside the garage. She liked to think that if anyone was lurking around that area, she'd see them because of that light.

It was probably more fantasy than reality, but it made her feel better.

The sound of her rubber soled shoes hitting the concrete and echoing around her was interrupted only briefly by the metallic sound of her keys bouncing off the tiny pepper spray can that dangled off her keychain. Tightly grasping her keys and the pepper spray, she quickly walked toward her car, her eyes darting left and right to see if anyone hid in the shadows.

Her heart pounded with every step so by the time she reached her driver's side door, her hands shook in fear. Taking one last look around, she pressed the key fob and saw the locks pop up inside the car doors. She quickly got in and relocked the doors as she breathed a sigh of relief.

All that stress for nothing, she thought, shaking her head at her foolishness.

Easing her vice-like grip on the car keys, she stuck one in the ignition and turned the engine on, causing the pepper spray canister to knock against the steering column and make a hollow, metallic noise. But another noise caught her attention, and in a split second she looked up to see the horrible face of a strange man staring back at her in the rearview mirror.

Terrified, her heart slammed into her chest as she scrambled to grab the pepper spray on her keychain, but before she could, he reached around the seat and clamped his hand over her mouth, forcing her back against the headrest. She couldn't breathe, and the smell of gasoline coating his hands filled her nose. She fought him, tearing at his thick, meaty fingers with her own knowing her life depended on it, but only for a few seconds before something hard hit her in the side of the head, and then everything faded to black.

✧ ✧ ✧

NICK HANSON SAT back in his chair and blew the air out of his lungs. The cards he held in his hand didn't impress him, but he needed to win back some of the money he'd lost in the past hour. Around the table sat the usual group of men he played poker with a few times a month. They'd been a group of ten at one point, but between marriage and work assignments, tonight they were down to seven.

"Those cards aren't going to get better just by

you staring at them, Nick."

He looked up and glared across the table at Xavier, a hacker he'd worked with in the bureau. Too cocky for his own good and younger than everyone else playing, he routinely pushed Nick's patience, especially when they played poker.

Looking over his cards, Nick frowned. "Smart ass. Are you in a hurry or something?"

Xavier grinned. "In fact, I have a date later tonight. I'm looking forward to using your money to entertain the young lady."

Next to him, Hunter threw his head back and laughed. The former LA detective enjoyed busting the hacker's ass any chance he got. "You better hurry, Nick. The blow up doll store will be closing soon."

Xavier snapped his head to his left and scowled. "Fuck you, man. When was the last time you got laid anyway? I'm betting it wasn't even in this century."

Nick watched in amusement as they shared insults. Even though Hunter had a few years on Xavier, nearly twenty years sounded like a long fucking time to go without sex. As their ass busting got nastier, he silently calculated that Hunter not having sex since the twentieth century would put him somewhere in his mid-teens the last time he got laid.

Hunter shook his head after Xavier once more

made a crack about his sex life. "You have a strange obsession with me fucking, dude."

To Nick's right, Gideon came to Xavier's defense, like usual. "You were the one who brought up the sex doll. Seems to me you have sex on the mind. Is it because you aren't getting any?"

A Navy Seal and expert in hand-to-hand combat, Gideon had left the service a year ago. Lately, he'd spent his time working with Nick on his cases and being as big a ballbuster as his buddy Xavier. A few years older than the hacker, he always joined him when he started busting chops.

Hunter rolled his eyes, knowing better than to spar with both of them. "I have no problem talking about who I'm fucking, but something tells me it's just the two of you who are obsessed with where everyone else's dick is going every night."

He looked over to his left and smiled at Roman. Of all the men around the table, Nick knew for a fact that he had no interest in Xavier and Gideon's sex obsession. An Army Ranger, he tended to say little, preferring actions to words. At the moment, the grimace that twisted his expression told everyone he didn't give a single fucking damn about talking sex during their card game.

"Whose turn is it to bet?" Roman asked, clearly wanting to return the focus to poker.

"Nick's," Xavier quickly answered, pointing at him. "He's just hoping his cards get better if he holds them longer."

Collapsing them into a single pile, Nick shook his head. "Fold."

"And the reason you couldn't say that five minutes ago?" Gideon asked in disgust as he threw a red chip into the center of the table. "Raise."

"Fuck you," Nick said, folding his arms across his chest. "You've gotten to be a royal pain in the ass since you met Xavier. You know that?"

Gideon laughed and waved off his claim. "When did you get so damn sensitive, Nick?"

Seated next to him, Marius tossed two more chips out. "Your five and up five. And get off Nick's back. We could always go to your shithole apartment and expect you to play host with the fucking most."

Nearly as serious as Roman, Marius, ex-CIA, shed his spook vibe when they all got together and liked to poke at Gideon and Xavier when they got going.

Standing from the table, Nick gave him a nod and a smile as Gideon chafed at his comment about his place. A typical bachelor, his apartment offered little more than four walls and a bed. They'd tried moving the game to other places, but after trying Gideon's practically empty rooms and

Hunter's condo in a building nearly an hour away from D.C., they all decided Nick's place in Georgetown with a poker table and enough room to fit them all worked best.

"Deal me out," Nick said as he headed for the couch. Maybe if he sat out a few hands his luck would return.

He grabbed the remote and pointed it at the TV. Tilting his head back, he listened to some show as he stared up at the ceiling above him. Bits and pieces of words from the TV and the men behind him floated into his head, but nothing sounded very interesting.

As the hand ended and Gideon celebrated a win with his usual gloating, Nick's phone vibrated in his pants pocket. Startled, he fished it out and looked at the screen through bleary eyes, not recognizing the number. Who the hell was calling him at just after ten at night?

He answered it curtly. "Hello." Unlike the way most people made it sound like a question, when the word came out of his mouth this time, it sounded more like an angry utterance.

"Hello, Mr. Hanson? Mr. Nick Hanson?" a deep voice asked in a cultured way that made even those common words sound important.

"This is him," he answered, even more tersely than he'd said hello.

"Mr. Hanson, my name is Marshall Gilmore.

I've been told you're just the man I should hire for a job I have," the man said confidently, as if they'd already struck a deal on this job of his.

"Oh, yeah? Why's that?"

A long moment of silence hung in the air before Marshall Gilmore answered flatly, "Because I'm told you're the man to call when you need someone to go undercover."

Nick sat up straight on the couch and focused on the TV as the man's statement bounced around in his head. That's who he'd been for years in the FBI, but he hadn't had a case like that in far too long. Long enough that he'd turned to seeking out family members for old rich ladies to supplement his bank account.

Maybe wishes did come true after all.

"You've got my attention, Mr. Gilmore. What do you say we meet tomorrow and talk about this job of yours you think I might want?"

"I don't have that long to wait. My daughter's been kidnapped and gone for a week. The FBI can't seem to find its ass with both hands, so I'd like you to come to see me tonight. If you're wondering if this is worth your while, I'm paying three hundred thousand dollars to get my daughter back, and if you get her back safely, I assure you for the rest of your life you'll see a handsome benefit from it."

For that amount of money, he'd take a drive to this guy's house and hear what he had to say.

Nick hadn't had a kidnapping case in ages, so the job already intrigued him.

"Okay. What's the address?"

Marshall Gilmore gave him the information and then said, "Mr. Hanson, I can't bear the thought of my daughter being hurt. They've had her for too long already. I don't want to lose her to these people."

"Give me a few minutes to get ready and I'll be there within the hour," Nick said as he stood from the couch to find his shoes.

"Thank you. When you get to the gate, tell the guard there your name. He'll know to let you in."

The phone went dead, and Nick stuffed it back into his pocket before searching for where his tie had landed hours before when he threw it off before the card game. As he did, he wondered who this Marshall Gilmore was to have a hundred grand to throw around and a guard with a gate protecting his house.

Whoever he was, he'd just made his night.

From behind him, he heard Marius say in a low voice, "Something tells me our guy Nick just got a new job."

Nick turned around and smiled. "Someone's got to pay for all this splendor. We don't want to end up hanging out at Gideon's and sitting on cardboard boxes, do we?" he joked.

Chapter Two

NICK STOOD IN an entryway that looked about the size of his entire apartment. Above him hung an enormous wrought iron chandelier he hoped was anchored properly. He shuffled his feet across the white Italian marble floor just in case that huge thing hanging overhead suddenly came crashing down, but a deep voice focused his attention on someone standing just outside the door to a room across the foyer.

"Mr. Hanson, please come in," a tall, grey haired man wearing a dark three-piece suit said as he waved him toward where he stood.

He did as asked and followed him into a bigger room with dark wood bookcases that rose to the ceiling and took up both the left and right walls. A massive bank of windows made up almost the entire outside wall ahead of him. Everything around him seemed enormous.

Marshall Gilmore extended his arm to offer him a chair in front of the biggest desk Nick had ever seen. Entire villages in Third World countries could eat on that desk. The chairs in front of the desk seemed small in comparison. As he took a seat, he ran his hand along the brown leather arm rest and gold nail heads that made the piece of furniture look sturdy, if not large.

"I'm glad you agreed to come out tonight," Marshall Gilmore said in a tone that made Nick feel that he had always expected him to do just that and his statement was a mere pleasantry to begin their conversation. "I get the feeling you don't know who I am, Mr. Hanson. Is that true?"

Unsure if he wanted to admit that truth, Nick quickly scanned the room for any sign of who Marshall Gilmore was and why he should know him. Unfortunately, he found nothing in the stacks of books around him and on the desk in front of him.

He shook him head. "Sorry, I don't. Should I?"

Leaning back in his chair, Marshall Gilmore nodded. "Not to put too fine a point on it, but yes, you should. If you've ever watched television in any part of this country or read a major newspaper on either of the coasts, you've met me in some small way. I'm the owner and CEO of Newscom America, the largest media conglomerate in the United States. When news happens in this country, my company brings it to the

American people."

That explained the mansion, security guards at the gate, and the wealth exhibited everywhere around him. It also explained how Marshall Gilmore could drop three hundred grand and not bat an eyelash. Nick had to admit he was impressed.

Regardless, he jumped right in and asked, "So the FBI is unable to handle the case? Why?"

Gilmore grimaced and shook his head. "I have no idea. It is their job, after all, but Persephone's been gone a week and they have no more clues than they had when this all started."

Persephone.

Nick hadn't liked too many subjects in literature class, but he had taken a shining to Greek mythology. The irony that someone had named their daughter after the goddess Hades kidnapped and forced to live in the Underworld and now that very girl had been kidnapped wasn't lost on him. He had a feeling her father wouldn't enjoy that irony, though, so he didn't bother to mention it.

"How old is your daughter, Mr. Gilmore?" he asked as he scanned the desk in front of him for any pictures of a small child.

He handed him an eight by ten picture of the girl, and for a moment, Nick stared at it in shock. Persephone Gilmore wasn't a child. She was a gorgeous adult woman. Posing alone for the camera, she stood outside the mansion he now sat in wearing a strapless black gown with her long brown hair flowing over her tanned shoulders. Even as she smiled, she looked like a perfect mixture of sexy and sweet, with dark brown doe eyes that made her look innocent and vulnerable.

"She's twenty-eight. She was taken by a group calling themselves the National Equality Militia last Tuesday night in a parking garage at the Christie Medical Center just outside of Front Royal. I don't know what the hell their problem is. Probably just another bunch of crackpots who don't want to work and want people like me to give them handouts. They contacted us with their demands and I immediately sent them exactly what they wanted."

Nick tore his attention away from the picture of the beautiful woman's face that sat in his lap and looked across the desk at her father. "How much did they want?"

"Five hundred thousand. I paid the day they told me to—Thursday morning—just like they said to in a black hard shell suitcase left outside a hotel in Alexandria just before nine a.m."

"And the FBI didn't catch them picking up the money?" Nick asked, confused they hadn't been able to handle that.

Gilmore shook his head. "No. They found

half a dozen people at that hotel who had suitcases just like it, but the one with the money in it somehow slipped through their hands."

Nick had seen this happen before, and it usually didn't mean a happy ending for the person who'd been taken. Once the kidnappers got their money, they had no use for the hostage anymore, so they often killed them.

"Have you spoken to your daughter since then?" he asked, afraid he'd have to be the one to explain to this father that if he hadn't, she likely wasn't alive anymore.

That would explain why the FBI didn't seem to have done their job like he wanted them to. Once that money got into the bad guys' hands, this became a completely different case.

But Gilmore nodded and sighed before answering, "Yes. She called just tonight. I know you probably thought they'd killed her after getting the money, but they say they want more. Another five hundred thousand."

"Will you pay it?"

"I'll pay anything, Mr. Hanson. Anything to get my daughter back. Look around you. Five hundred thousand is a drop in the bucket compared to what I have, and I'd give my last cent to have Persephone back safely. But I don't think the FBI can do it. That's why I called you. I've been told you're the man who can take care of this. I'm told your past experience makes you the perfect man for this job, in fact. Because this isn't just about finding her and then telling the FBI. This is about finding her and getting her out of the hands of these maniacs. I want someone who can do that and do it fast. Is that you?"

Nick didn't have to think twice about his answer. Yes, he was the man Marshall Gilmore needed to find and rescue his daughter from whatever this National Equality Militia was. He'd gone undercover more times than he could remember when he was with the bureau, so yes, he could find Persephone Gilmore and get her away from her captors.

"A hundred grand and you tell no one you hired me. I don't need the FBI getting in my way, and that's exactly what they'll do if you tell them I'm working for you, Mr. Gilmore."

Shaking his head, he frowned. "Fine. They seem more focused on the idea that my daughter is some airheaded debutante out cruising around with this month's bad boys anyway after the kidnappers sent those pictures to my competitors. I have no compunction to tell them much of anything."

"What pictures? Did the kidnappers send pictures of your daughter?"

Marshall Gilmore looked confused for a moment at Nick's ignorance about the pictures and then handed them across the desk with a look of disgust on his face. "They think this shows she's not a prisoner at all. I told them to go to hell. I know my daughter, Mr. Hanson. She isn't some poor little rich girl looking for excitement. She's a nurse, for God's sake. She's devoted her adult life to helping people. She's the most honorable person I know, and to say it looks like she's having a good time—"

His voice caught on that last word, and Nick looked up from the pictures of Persephone Gilmore at what appeared to be some farm sitting outside on a hay bale and seeming to be as happy as a clam. He wondered if her father might be wrong about how honorable she actually was since the pictures looked pretty damning.

"None of your competitors know where the pictures came from?"

"No."

"What about how they got here? Courier? Anything that can be traced?" Nick asked.

Marshall Gilmore shook his head. "No. They were left at the guard shack in the middle of the night. Goddamn cowards."

"If they threatened her, they could get her to do anything they wanted," Nick said, trying to be supportive as he considered the possibility that this whole case was simply some bored socialite just trying to have fun.

Then again, why would she have some people calling themselves a militia demand money from her own father? Or was it a case that daddy held the purse strings too tight?

"Does your daughter have money of her own?"

Marshall Gilmore nodded. "More than enough for most people, I would say. She draws from a trust fund each year that pays for anything she could want."

"Then why didn't they just take that money?" Nick asked, hoping to get Gilmore to give more details about this trust fund.

"It can't all be taken out at once. It's meant to give her money for years, not to be blown all at once. It's how my grandfather did it for his children, how my father did it for my brothers and sisters and me, and it's how I did it for my three daughters. Anyone who wants a large sum of money would have to come to me."

"Has anyone come to you for a large sum of money recently? Anyone you turned down perhaps? Anyone who would be desperate enough to kidnap your daughter?"

"No. They say this is to fund their anti-media, anti-wealth militia. It sounds like a bunch of utter nonsense to me, but then again, I'd never heard of any of them until last week when they kidnapped my daughter."

"Let me see anything else they sent you. A letter, perhaps, explaining why they took her and their demands?"

Frowning, Gilmore shook his head. "The FBI has it. All I know is they don't like money or the media, and I'm both. Now, can you get her back for me, Mr. Hanson?"

Nick nodded. "I'll get her back for you."

He took one last look at the picture of Persephone Gilmore in his lap and silently promised her he'd do whatever it took to get her home safely to her family. Something about the kindness in her eyes made him want to protect her, and no bullshit militia group with delusions of changing the world was going to stop him.

A FEW CALLS to friends who worked cases like he did got him little more on the National Equality Militia other than the question of who the hell they were, and as he opened up his laptop to search for details on the group, Nick wondered if they were actually anything at all. A tiny voice in the back of his mind began to doubt Marshall Gilmore's story. Or maybe it was his daughter's story that didn't ring true.

Whichever it was, before he could begin the case, he needed to know what he would be walking into and who the hell these militia people were.

He typed their name into the search bar, expecting to find at least a page of articles and sites about them. What he got was three listings and then a bunch of results about other groups with similar names.

As he clicked on the first article, he mumbled, "Some bunch of revolutionaries. I guess that's what you get when your main goal is equality. Nobody gives a damn about that anymore."

Scanning the page, he found out the group's main beliefs. They had some problem with wealthy people making more money and media companies making money or some idiotic notion like that. Nick rolled his eyes. The foolishness of groups like these never ceased to amaze him. People made money. It wasn't a crime. Well, not usually, and when it was, the authorities found out and made them pay. Sometimes in jail time, and sometimes in money.

Railing against people making money seemed a ridiculous thing to organize around, but as he continued to read about how they'd staged protests outside major news corporation buildings in New York and Los Angeles, he had to grudgingly admit they seemed sincere in their intentions.

But now that sincerity had taken a wrong turn into fanatical with the kidnapping of Persephone

Gilmore. Marching in front of office buildings with picket signs was one thing. Taking the daughter of the most powerful media magnate in the country was an entirely different thing.

Zeroing in on the images of the people in the militia, he saw one common thread. All white guys. Angry white guys hating the world for what it had done to them.

He'd fit right in.

✧   ✧   ✧

AFTER GETTING A tip from an old friend who worked in counterterrorism in the D.C. Metropolitan Police that some of the militia's supporters liked to hang out at a dive bar called Trusser's in Manassas, Nick headed down there dressed in his oldest jeans, a faded black t-shirt, and shit kicker work boots he found in the back of his closet. He hadn't worn them since one of the first jobs he did after leaving the FBI when he had to go undercover as a gardener to find out who was stalking his client. They still felt like fifty pound weights every time he lifted his feet to walk, just as they had years ago on that case, and they made his gait look way cockier than usual as he made his way to the end of the bar.

The bartender with a ratty beard and pot belly walked over to stand in front of him and gave Nick a look like he felt put out having to wait on him. "What do you want to drink?"

He glanced down the bar at the taps and answered, "Give me a Grant's Tomb."

Not a beer drinker, he nonetheless liked the name of the beer he saw on the tap. It reminded him of that old joke about who was buried in Grant's tomb.

A few seconds later, the man set a glass of amber colored liquid down in front of him and walked away. Nick took a drink, instantly decided it was the worst thing he'd ever had in his mouth, and looked around the bar to see if any of the militia's supporters were there.

It didn't take him long to find them. In the area behind him, two men stood shooting a game of pool and talking about the group's goals and how they hoped they'd finally show the world how bad it had become because of the people in power and their love of money.

Nick turned around on the barstool and saw the two of them as they finished their game. Both looked like they'd come straight from a neo-Nazi meeting. Hair buzzed close to their heads, dressed in all black with black boots, they had a paramilitary look to them that he'd seen in pictures of the National Equality Militia online.

Sliding off the barstool, he took a breath and put himself into his role. Angry white guy ready to rage at the world. As he walked toward them, he said to himself, "Now to find out where these motherfuckers are and find Persephone."

Before he reached them, one of them tossed his pool cue onto the table in disgust and said, "We need to find more people like us, man. The movement can't die. We just can't let those fucks win."

That's all he needed to hear. A few well-chosen words would be all it would take with these two. Not exactly great thinkers, they wouldn't even stop to wonder who he was or why he wanted to join their group.

"You guys want to shoot a game?" Nick asked as he picked up the pool stick.

The two men looked at one another and then back at him. "Yeah, sure. You look like someone we can hang with."

As the shorter one racked the balls, he looked across the pool table and said, "What's your name? You from around here?"

"Nick and I'm from Warrenton."

"Oh yeah?" the other one said, suddenly far more interested in him than he was before.

With a smile, Nick said, "Yeah. I guess you can say we're best known for being the birthplace of no less than ten Confederate generals. Rebels through and through."

The man at the other end of the table took his first shot and made a shitty break with only four balls trickling out of the triangle. If he'd been there to hustle pool, these two would be perfect marks. As it was, Nick didn't give a damn about the game. He had bigger goals than taking a few bucks off these two assholes, so he kept their focus on the idea of rebellion instead of how bad the guy's break had been.

"I heard what you guys were talking about while I was walking over. You're damn right about not letting those motherfuckers win. They're turning this world into shit for guys like us. Someone needs to stop them before it gets to the point that we can't anymore."

"Damn fucking straight!" the man who wasn't playing said as he lifted his fist in the air. "Guys like us have to fight back or they're going to make slaves out of us."

Nick took his shot, intentionally only making one ball into a pocket instead of the two he could have, and nodded. "Fucking right. It's time to rise the fuck up, man."

He knew exactly what to say and how to say it. The eager way both of them agreed with him told Nick it wouldn't take more than a single game of pool before he was in their club of angry white guys who wanted to change the world so only they benefited.

"Talk is cheap, man," his pool partner said as he took another shitty shot and sent a ball careening off the side of the table into a group of his balls but getting nothing in any pocket. "What guys like us need to do is act. You ready to act or are you all talk and no action, man?"

Eyeing up his next shot, Nick smiled. "The time for talking is over."

As the cue ball raced across the table into one of his balls, sending it into the corner pocket, the guy watching moved over to pat him on the back. "Then let's get going. We have some people you should meet."

Nick tossed the pool stick on the table and nodded. "Hell yeah. Let's start changing this fucking world."

Chapter Three

T HIRTEEN DAYS. ONE long, awful, terrifying week followed by six more horrible days.

Persephone stretched her mouth to relieve the pain of the gag one of her captors had forced onto her while another tied a rope around her hands behind her back, around her ankles, and her waist to hold her to the old wooden chair they kept her in day and night for the whole time they'd held her. The rope tore at the delicate skin on her wrists every time she moved. If only she could just sit still, but every fiber of her being screamed day and night she needed to move.

That she needed to do whatever she could to escape from these men.

They'd taken her to that farm and ordered her at gunpoint to dance around that pasture like some frolicking fairy loving life out in the country. Her legs nearly gave out half a dozen times, weak from fear as her whole body shook in terror while they barked out orders for her to look happier and to smile bigger.

"Look like you're fucking loving this, bitch!" they screamed as she ran around in the green grass hoping someone somewhere could see her and how terrified she truly was.

That had been the only time they let her off that horrible old wooden chair, except when she begged them to let her use the bathroom. A half hour feeling the sun on her face out of nearly two weeks held against her will by them.

She still had no idea who they were. All she knew about the men who came into the room with her was they were young, white, and angrier than anyone else she'd never met in her life. She didn't know if all of them where they held her were as angry as the ones who tended to her, but the four or five she'd met so far made her believe that one wrong move and she'd end up dead.

That is, dead before the moment they intended to kill her.

Persephone had seen enough news in her life to know how this would end. They'd kidnapped her to extract money from her father. When they got it, they'd have no more use for her. That's how this went.

She knew her father well enough to know that he'd hand over any amount to get her back. Marshall Gilmore may have been cutthroat in business, but when it came to his family, he'd move heaven and earth for his daughters and wife.

But just as she knew the reality of her situation, he did too and maybe he wouldn't give them the ransom quickly. He hadn't made his fortune by being outsmarted by others. Maybe he'd try to bargain with them. She wasn't what they wanted. Surely, they wanted money more than her. The problem was she didn't know if that would help her or hurt her.

Holding back tears at how much everything hurt as she sat there tied to that chair for more than half a day since her last bathroom trip, she looked around at the room they held her in. Nondescript white walls that looked like they were covered in plaster made her think the building was older. Beneath her, a worn hardwood floor reinforced that belief.

Was she being held in a house? She knew they'd moved her after the farm trip, but she'd been gagged, blindfolded, and bound, so she couldn't even guess where they'd taken her to. Nothing the men around her said gave her any clue as to where they were. In fact, they said little at all, and when they did speak, it was mostly to threaten her to keep quiet and stop crying.

Which she did a lot of.

She wasn't ashamed of that either. She had every right to be scared for her life, and she'd seen enough patients in the hospital break down when they found out their cases were terminal.

And that's exactly what her case was.

Terminal.

These men wouldn't let her live much longer. Once they got what they wanted, they'd get rid of her.

So she had to find a way out and now.

SLOWLY, SHE LIFTED her head and opened her eyes to look around at the room in front of her. With the windows blacked out, she couldn't tell if it was day or night. She listened for sounds from her captors and heard voices talking low somewhere nearby in the building. Their conversation made no sense, mainly because she only heard a few words every so often, but she tried to understand what they said in the hopes that it might help her escape from this wretched place.

Footsteps coming toward where she sat made her heart slam against her chest, and for the hundredth time, Persephone prayed to God this wouldn't be the one when they pressed the end of a gun to her head and pulled the trigger.

The door opened behind her, creaking on its hinges in the way it did every time. It never failed to send chills down her spine as that ominous sound hit her ears.

She craned her neck to see which one it was.

The one with the crew cut and tattoos of a skull and crossbones on his face? Or the one with slightly longer dark hair and eyes that harbored such rage she worried each time he appeared that he'd unleash that horrible anger on her?

The one with the brown hair pulled back into a ponytail who sneered in that terrifying way every time he had to come in to feed her or take her to the bathroom?

Or worst of all, the one who always pointed his gun directly at her as she swallowed spoonful after spoonful of that awful food they forced on her. They all liked to let her know they carried guns, but he went beyond using his to warn her.

The pleased look in his nearly black eyes said he got off terrifying her with that gun of his.

Oh God! It was the one with the gun!

"Time to eat, bitch," he said, practically growling at her.

In his eyes, she saw the hate he felt for her. It terrified Persephone more than anything she'd ever encountered in her life.

This time he wasn't alone, though. Behind him followed a man she hadn't seen before. Dark haired, he wore it short but not shaved to his head. He had an angular face and little scruff, but he didn't look dirty like the others. Overall, he didn't look very much like a revolutionary, as the rest of his friends like to call themselves.

Persephone watched as the one with the gun handed him the bowl of whatever terrible food he'd brought to feed her. "On second thought, you feed this bitch. Why should I get stuck with this fucking slave shit?"

The new man simply shrugged. "Fine. I'll feed her. What is this shit anyway?"

Surprised by the question, the one with the gun made a face of disgust. "How the fuck do I know? I'm not a fucking cook. She needs to be fed so she doesn't starve to death on us, so this is what we're feeding her. You writing a book? Make this one a fucking mystery."

Again, the new man shrugged. "Whatever. Just making conversation."

Waving his gun, the angry one stopped and pointed it at Persephone's head. "Don't let her give you any fucking attitude. If she does, smack her. She needs to learn her place."

A smile spread across the new man's face. "Got it. Anything else?"

"Don't listen to her if she says she has to go to the bathroom. She just took a piss a few hours ago."

He glared at her and made a gesture like he shot the gun and it kicked back in his hand before storming out and slamming the door behind him. Left alone with her, the new guy set the bowl of slop he needed to feed her on the table across the room and picked up a chair in one hand, swinging it around him as he grabbed the bowl again. The motion looked fluid, like he had done it a million times.

He set the chair down in front of her and with one hand untied the gag from behind her head, letting it fall away to the floor. As he sat down, Persephone stretched her mouth and closed her eyes to revel in the brief respite from that terrible pain the gag inflicted on her jaw.

"Are you hungry?" the man asked in a low voice barely above a whisper.

She opened her eyes and stared at him in amazement. No one had spoken to her like that in the thirteen days she'd been their hostage. In fact, no one had asked her a single question since they brought her there. Her comfort or anything about her didn't interest them in the least.

As she looked at him, she couldn't help but notice how different he seemed from the other men she'd met from the group. His dark brown eyes held no true anger toward her, and nothing in his expression said he wanted to kill her.

But she knew how quickly that could change with these men, and she had no reason to doubt he wasn't just like them.

Cruel. Vicious. Deadly.

And no matter how gentle his eyes appeared now, when he held his gun to her head and threatened to pull the trigger because she'd upset him by doing something insignificant, he'd be as terrifying as the others.

"Well, hungry or not, I have to feed you, so open up your mouth," he said in a tone that sounded almost amused.

What could be funny to him she had no idea.

He lifted the spoon from what looked like a grey version of oatmeal and brought it to her mouth, but she closed her lips tightly and shook her head. Whatever that shit in the bowl was, she didn't want any. She suspected they were drugging her food to make her more compliant anyway. She didn't feel like helping them with that since being on her toes might be the only way to escape this place and them.

The man watched her as she refused the food he offered and smiled. "Neither of us really has a choice here, so why not make it easy on both of us and eat?"

What the hell was he smiling for?

Enraged at his cavalier attitude toward her as she sat tied to a chair with her hands bound behind her back, she snapped, "Stop smiling! I'm a prisoner here. See the ropes around my hands? There's nothing funny about that. And I'm not going to make anything easy on you just so you or one of your thug friends can kill me a day or two from now."

Immediately, she regretted her outburst and waited for the inevitable pain that would come when he smacked her across the face as the man who fed her the first night did when she protested. She hadn't made that mistake again, but something about this one's stupid smiling had pushed her past the point of reason.

Looking away, she braced herself and waited with dread for the painful sting of being hit, but instead, he quietly said, "I'm sorry. I forgot myself for a minute there. It happens sometimes when you're playing a part. I'm not going to punish you for what you said, but I do have to feed you."

Persephone listened to him speak like a normal, completely not psychotic person and turned to face him again. "Who are you? Why are you being so nice to me?"

His dark gaze slid over her, down from her eyes to her lips and then her neck where she knew there were bruises from when one of their hands had painfully pushed against her tender skin and left it purple and ugly. A feeling of shame washed over her as he stared for too long at the evidence that she'd been attacked by one of the men, and she turned away again to avoid his knowing glance when he lifted his eyes to look into hers.

"I'm sorry they did that to you," he said quietly.

Even more stunned from this second apology

than she'd been at the first, she looked at him and shook her head in disbelief. "What's your game? I know you're no different than any of the others, so are you trying to lure me into a feeling of false security so when you hit me you get some kind of bigger rush? Just do it because I'm not falling for this nice guy thing you're trying to do."

The man said nothing for a long moment, making Persephone sure that at any second the swift retribution for what she dared say would come down on her. No matter what he wanted her to believe, she knew better.

He may have looked kinder, but no decent man would be anywhere near the men holding her hostage. No, this man was just as dangerous as any of the others.

"My name is Nick. I can't say much more without putting both of us in danger, but you can trust me. I won't let them hurt you, Persephone."

This man—this Nick—spoke as if he knew her and cared about her. But how could that be? He was one of them. She wouldn't be fooled by his gentle words and kind eyes.

No matter how desperate she was deep in her soul to believe everything he offered in those words and eyes.

"I don't know who you are or who you think you're fooling, Nick, but if you think for a second I'm falling for this act of yours, forget it. If any good resided inside you, then you wouldn't be within a mile of these guys."

Her indictment of him didn't seem to faze the man one bit, though. He simply nodded and smiled again, like any of what was going on between them or around them was anything to crack a smile about.

"Do you enjoy my pain, Nick? Is that why you keep smiling?" Persephone asked, her anger with his amusement at the situation once again making her braver than she should have been.

And yet, once again, he didn't hit her. He didn't do anything, except for take that infuriating smile off his face.

"I'm not happy with what's happening to you. I'm smiling because I'm glad you're a fighter. If you were some pathetic thing who wasn't intent on fighting for her life, this would be much harder. That's all the smile is about. I'm not trying to make light of what you're going through."

Confused, Persephone narrowed her eyes and stared at him to try to figure out what this guy's plan was. Did he intend on making her think he could be her ally just to betray her to those devils outside that room? To what end? What could he get from her that could be of any use to him?

"I don't know what you're doing, but I'm not going to fall for it. And I don't want any of that grey gruel you keep scooping onto that spoon either, so don't even try to feed that to me because I promise you'll end up wearing it."

Nick lowered his head, but she saw he was trying to hide his smile. Again with the damn smiling!

"You think what I said was funny?"

Looking up at her, he shook his head. "I don't know how you expect me to keep a straight face when you say things like that. What kind of hostage talks to her captors like that? I clearly need to work on my bad guy vibe because it's not coming through with you, for sure."

"You're here to play head games with me, aren't you? You do seem a lot smarter than the rest of them, so I guess you're a good choice for the job, but I'm not some stupid debutante who's never seen anything of the horrors of life, so whatever you think you're doing, it's not going to work."

"Head games?" he asked, acting like what she said confused him.

But she knew better. He may have been far less of a Cro-Magnon man than the rest of his friends, but he was no rocket scientist. That she was sure of.

And he wasn't very convincing in this innocent thing he tried to convey.

"You're probably doing some good cop-bad

cop thing with one of your buddies out there. Maybe that one who likes to press the end of his gun to the side of my face whenever he feeds me. He's the bad guy, and you're the good guy. You make me think I'm not going to die in this place, and then that bastard comes in and shows me just how wrong I was to believe in you."

She shook her head, refusing to fall for the trick. "Nope. Sorry. Just be man enough to kill me yourself if that's the way it's going to be. Don't leave it up to him. He'd probably get off on it anyway, so why give that guy all the good stuff?"

"I'm not here to play any games with you. Right now, I just need to get some of this food into you so you don't starve to death. Can you at least try a spoonful of this stuff for me?"

Staring at him in utter disbelief, she asked, "Why are you acting like we're friends or something here? I'm not going to try anything for you, Nick. You're holding me hostage, for God's sake! My hands are tied behind my back for so long my shoulders are killing me. I guess that's better than real death, so thanks for that, but I'm a prisoner here. Stop trying to act like we're friends because we're not."

With each word, her voice rose until she was practically screaming by the time she finished. Whatever he'd been sent in there to do—twist her thoughts with his mind games, play good cop to the rest of their bad cop routine, or whatever other horrible thing he intended—she wasn't going to let it happen without fighting it.

Her yelling made his eyes fill with fear, and he turned to look at the door like he expected someone to come busting in at any second. Looking back at her, he put his finger to his lips and whispered, "Don't yell. If you do, they'll come in and I don't know what they'll do. I'm not trying to hurt you. I'm trying to help you here. You don't have to believe me, but for the moment, at least give me the benefit of the doubt."

"Why? Why should I do that?" she asked, unsure what this man was trying to do to her.

He took a deep breath and let it out slowly. "Because I'm here to save you. I can't do that if they decide it's time to kill you."

"You're here to save me?" she asked as his words repeated in her brain.

Save her? Why would this person do that? Why would he betray his fellow militia men who kidnapped her?

"Yes, and even though I'm happy you're a fighter because you're going to need that when we escape from these people, that fighting isn't going to help you with them now. They hate women, or at least they hate your kind of woman, so fighting will only make them want to take out their rage on you. I know you don't know me, but trust me. I'm here to help."

What he said settled into her mind until she thought maybe it made sense, so she asked, "Are you a cop? FBI? Are you doing some kind of undercover thing here?"

She wanted to believe he might be telling the truth. The tiny spark of hope inside her had flickered until it nearly extinguished itself in the past few days of her captivity, but now it leapt inside her at the mere thought that maybe she might make it out alive with his help.

Whispering in her ear, he said, "I'm not a cop or FBI. Your father hired me to rescue you, and that's what I intend on doing. I just need you to trust me."

"I don't believe you. My father wouldn't wait all this time to send someone."

There was no damn way this guy was telling the truth. Her father wouldn't make her suffer for nearly two weeks. No way.

"He didn't. When he decided the FBI wasn't seeing this case like they should, he called me. That was last week."

"Then why didn't you show up until today?"

"I had to get in with them, which took a few days. They aren't exactly the most trusting people on Earth. Now listen to me. This could get ugly, and I'm talking really ugly. I need you to remember that whatever happens, I won't let them hurt you. I promise. I won't let them hurt you, Persephone. But if it does get as ugly as it could get, I need you to remember I'm doing this to save you. Never forget that, okay?"

Nick leaned away, settling his gaze directly on her. What did he mean by as ugly as it could get if he wasn't going to let them hurt her? What was going to happen that made his warning sound so chilling?

Reason told her not to trust this man. He was one of them. But hope made her want to believe what he said, and at that moment, she chose to hope that he wasn't simply toying with her for some sick and perverted enjoyment he'd get later when he told her it had all been a lie.

For now, she'd trust this Nick. What other choice did she have?

Chapter Four

NICK WATCHED AS Persephone considered whether to trust him or not, her eyes narrowing as she studied him. He understood her skepticism. Dressed like one of the men who held her hostage, he didn't exactly look like the kind of guy anyone should believe, especially at that moment as he sat in front of her while she remained bound at her wrists with a rope around her waist tying her to the chair. The fact that he appeared to be a part of the National Equality Militia didn't add any credibility to his claims.

He knew all that and still hoped she'd believe him. This job would be much harder if she didn't, and having the person you're trying to help fight you every step of the way never turned out good.

The bruises on her neck made him cringe in anger. Those fuckers had choked her at some point in addition to hitting her, if that discoloration under her eye was any indication. It wasn't bad enough they had to smack her around? They had to grab her like that too?

Instantly, that made him wonder what else they'd done to her. She had too much fight in her for them to have raped her. At least he wanted to believe that. The thought of them doing that to her made his stomach turn.

Lowering the bowl to his lap, he reached out to lightly touch the purple bruise just under her left ear. She flinched as his fingertip grazed her skin, wincing like it hurt to merely be touched.

"Does that hurt?" he asked as a way to try to get her to talk about what they'd done to her.

"No," she answered, obviously lying as she shrank from his touch every time his finger moved against her skin.

"I don't want to hurt you," he whispered, pulling his hand away. "Have they done anything else other than choke you and hit you?"

Silently, she shook her head, but her frown deepened.

"You can tell me. Honest. You can trust me, Persephone."

"They haven't done anything to me other than that. Not that I'd want to tell another human being if they had, but they haven't. I don't get the feeling they think of me as a sexual thing so much as goods they can trade for."

He knew all too well what people like this militia thought of women. He'd seen it time and time again. She was right. To them, women were things to be bought, sold, and traded for, but even worse, they didn't consider them people with feelings. If the mood came over one of them that made him want to prove his power over her, Nick didn't doubt for a moment that they'd rape her without a second thought.

"Don't let yourself get deluded, Persephone. This group has a special hatred for women. That hatred would justify just about anything they wanted to do to you."

He regretted sharing his inner thoughts because immediately fear filled her eyes. Quickly, he placed his hand on her shoulder to fix his mistake.

"I told you I won't let them hurt you. You don't have to worry. Okay?"

The fear in her dark eyes gave way to disbelief he knew it would take time to dissuade her of. He would, though. If it took everything he had inside, he would prove to her that she could believe in him. The job depended on that.

"Where are we?" she asked in a tiny voice so different from the one she used before with him. "Where have they taken me? Are we still in the United States? I know I've been held hostage for thirteen days, or at least I think I have, but I have little sense of where I am after the farm they took me to."

"You're at a house in a small town in Virginia.

Do you know why they took you to the farm?"

She shook her head and sighed. "I don't know why they kidnapped me at all. What's this about?"

Nick looked over toward the door to see if anyone was coming in and then turned his attention back to her. "The people who kidnapped you are the National Equality Militia. They seem to have some problems with people who make money, like your father, and the media having any ability to make money, also like your father."

She sneered at his explanation. "Equality? They call this equality, or is that only for angry white guys like them?"

Persephone had pegged them correctly. Nick continued, "I suspect only people like them are entitled to their brand of equality. They're angry about everything. From what I read about them, they claim that everyone else but them have been helped in this country and they were left behind. So they formed this group and started picketing news stations that didn't tell their story the way they wanted it told."

She frowned and shook her head. "The news is about the truth. Or at least it's supposed to be. That's what my father always believed anyway. Ironic that they took me, the daughter of the one man in the news business who demands his media tell the truth."

Scooping the grey, chunky liquid up into the spoon, Nick let it drop back into the bowl with a plop. "They aren't interested in anyone telling the truth. They just want people to hear their opinions and give them what they want. There's very little truth to what they believe. The fact that they can be unemployed and still afford to have all those guns and have the time and money to pull off an operation like this kidnapping shows they have pretty easy lives, comparatively speaking."

For the first time, Persephone smiled and Nick saw that beautiful woman he'd seen in the picture Marshall Gilmore had shown him. Only now, she sat in green scrubs she'd worn for weeks, her hair hung in a tangled mess down past her shoulders, and her face and neck had bruises that showed the misery she'd endured.

But still, she was beautiful.

"You don't sound much like a revolutionary, or whatever they think they are. You better work on that."

"Oh, don't worry. When you see me around any of them, you won't even recognize me. It'll be pretty damn horrifying, so brace yourself. And not like I was with that guy a few minutes ago. I just need you to remember that whatever I do, I'm doing it to save you. Don't forget that."

The smile slid from her expression at his

promise that he'd be just as evil as the men outside the room. For Nick, he knew what he had to do and he knew why he had to do it. He just didn't like how that truth made her look at him.

"I better get going before they think something is going on in here. I'll be back later to feed you dinner. Do you need to go to the bathroom?"

"No. But how do you know it will be you who has to feed me again?" she asked.

As he placed the bowl of slop on the table nearby, he smiled. "Because I'm the new guy and they think that's giving me the dirty job. Up is down in these people's world, I guess."

Turning back to face her, he knew he had to put the gag back on her, even if he didn't want to. The pretense had to be kept up or her captors might figure out he wasn't who he claimed he was and they'd both pay the price for that mistake.

He crouched down next to her to pick up the rag they'd used on her and stood up to stuff it into her mouth again. Holding the cloth in his hand, he looked at her and tried to soften the news the best he could.

"I have to put this back on you. I'm sorry," he said, hanging his head.

"Why? Couldn't you just forget? I've had that thing in my mouth every day and night. I have to breathe through my nose the whole time, which starts to really hurt after a while. Can't you just leave it off for now, and if someone comes in and sees, then you can just say you forgot to do it?" she pleaded.

He hated the answer he had to give her. He truly did, but neither of them could afford any slip up that might endanger them getting away from there alive.

Clutching the gag in his hand, he frowned. "I'm sorry. I am. But I have to do this."

She shook her head violently as he attempted to gently push it into her mouth, so he took hold of her head to stop her. Looking up at him with those deep brown eyes filled with complete and utter fear now, she begged one more time for him not to do it in a voice that made his chest hurt.

"Please. Nick, please. Don't do this. You want me to trust you, but how can I when you insist on sticking that thing back in my mouth?"

Damnit, he hated who he had to be sometimes.

"I have to. We can't afford for them to think that I'm treating you any better than they are. I promise that I'll come back before dinner, if I can, and remove it for as long as possible. I promise."

He held her head still as she tried to push back against his palm to escape what he had to do. The more she fought him, the more he wanted to stop and do as she so desperately wanted, but he didn't have a choice.

No matter how much he wished he did.

As gently as he could, he pushed the cloth into her mouth as she tried to push it out with her lips and then clamped down on his fingers with her teeth. She caught his forefinger and bit down hard, nearly drawing blood. Yanking his hand away, he shook it to ease the sting as she stared at him with hurt in her dark eyes that caused him more pain than any bite ever could.

"I'll be back. Remember what I said. Don't fight them. They'll hurt you if you do."

As he walked toward the door, he heard her say something that sounded like, "Like you just did."

In her eyes, he was no better than those bastards who'd hit her and choked her. Hopefully, gagging her would be the worst he'd have to do to her. But he wouldn't count on that.

THE MEN OF the National Equality Militia spent most of their time playing video games as far as Nick could tell in the day he'd been with them. When he left the room where they were holding Persephone, he walked directly into the group of five grown men arguing about whose turn it was to do whatever they did in the game that seemed to revolve around some kind of zombies taking over the world.

Or at least that's what it looked like as he moved through the room toward the kitchen with the bowl of food he hadn't gotten Persephone to take even a bite of in all his time with her. He hurried toward the sink to wash down the evidence of his failure to force her to eat. Dishes from at least two days of meals piled up on one side, while on the other side beer bottles sat soaking in water. He had no idea why any of them would be doing that, but he didn't care.

He just needed to get this grey shit down the drain before any of them saw how much was left in the bowl.

As he pushed aside the dirty plates crusted with egg from breakfast, he hurried to turn the water on and wash away everything in the bowl. Behind him, the heavy sound of footsteps told him someone planned to join him, so he pushed the spoon faster to get rid of it all into the drain.

"So how was your first time dealing with her?" the one everyone called Drist asked. "She's a real bitch, isn't she? I had to show her who's boss once or twice."

Nick took a deep breath of relief as all the grey oatmeal stuff disappeared and then turned around to see the man talking to him. Drist had light hair cut short to his head and far too many tattoos for any person to have on his neck and face. Any world that let this guy have control over anything was a world with serious problems since he obviously had made some extremely poor choices concerning his appearance.

Worst of all, though, was his obsession with that gun he waved around so much. Nick had been with them for just under a day, and in that time, Drist had used the handgun for everything from scratching his balls to punctuating his thoughts by pointing it at the person he was speaking to. Assuming he kept it loaded, Drist was definitely the most dangerous of all the militia men Nick had met so far.

He suspected Drist had been one of the men who had hurt Persephone. Any guy who needed to show off a gun as much as he did definitely had power issues with women. And other men. Hell, he probably had power issues with animals.

Before he could get lost in the horrific images forming in his head about what Drist had likely done to some poor kid's pets growing up, Nick forced himself to answer his questions.

"You know how bitches like her are. They're used to having everything given to them on a silver platter. She probably likes the idea that men are feeding her. I was thinking next time I might just put the bowl on the ground and let her eat like a fucking dog."

Drist's eyes lit up like he just heard the best

thing all day. "Do it! You'd just have to make sure her ankles stay tied so she couldn't get away, but I'd pay to see that bitch feeding like a dog."

Thankfully, he turned around to tell the rest of the men playing video games about the fantastic idea, leaving Nick alone. Either that guy had the tiniest dick in the world, or some woman had wrecked him bad in the past. Maybe he had some traumatic thing with his mother. Nick could see the guy having mommy issues. He didn't know what his problem was, but he silently vowed to keep him and the rest of the men away from Persephone as much as possible.

He couldn't avoid dealing with them, unfortunately, though. For him to get her out of there any time soon, he needed to know what they planned. That meant he had to strike up a conversation with at least one of them.

The ones he'd met at the bar who brought him there had left, probably to go recruit more willing volunteers to the militia's cause. That left Drist, who Nick never wanted to have to deal with, if he could help it, and four others who had done nothing but play on that X-Box since he got there earlier in the day.

Scanning the room, he tried to pick the one who looked the most civilized. It wasn't an easy choice. None of them looked like they'd win any prizes for being very bright or even decent. As he considered which one to speak to, the guy with the ponytail threw the game controller in his hands across the room toward the guy on the couch.

"Fuck this! Let those damn zombies eat you if you don't want to help me!" he barked before storming away toward the room where Persephone stayed.

Nick's body immediately went on red alert. He couldn't let that maniac go in there and terrorize her, so he quickly followed him. But instead of heading to that room, he marched down the hallway toward another bedroom all of them shared.

Relieved, Nick followed and saw him sitting on one of the old stained mattresses on the floor still stewing about how his buddy hadn't supported his zombie killing in the game. He mumbled something about the guy being a motherfucker or some other kind of fucker, and when he turned to see someone else coming into the room, he jumped up like he'd been startled.

"What the fuck do you want?" he snapped.

Christ, the anger came off him in waves. Maybe video game zombie hunting wasn't the best thing for him. Maybe some needlepoint might be better for this guy.

Nick held his hands up in front of him to let him know he meant no harm. "It's cool, man. I just came in here to get away from those fucking zombies."

For a moment, the ponytail guy stared like he didn't know whether or not to believe him, but then he nodded his agreement. "I know, right? Who needs that shit? Fucking zombies. It's not like they actually exist. Killing people is much easier anyway. That's the kind of game I want. A people killing game."

"Exactly. What the fuck do I care about killing creatures that eat fucking brains? Brains aren't for eating, crazy fuckers," Nick said with a chuckle.

Ponytail laughed a little too hard for his comfort, but at least he had him doing something other than throwing things and cursing out the living dead. Now he just needed to get him to talk about what the group's plans were.

Assuming he knew one damn thing about what those plans might be.

Chapter Five

"SO WHAT'S GOING on with all this?" Nick asked, motioning with his head toward the room where Persephone stayed. "What are we supposed to be doing with her?"

"Fuck if I know," Ponytail said with a grunt of disgust. "Clayton told us she was going to help us get the word out about what we're doing, but as far as I can tell, all she's done is sit in that room. I mean, why aren't we making videos of her so her daddy can put them all over his TV stations? That would get their attention."

Nick knew Clayton was the leader of the militia. Clayton Burger, a low level thief who had convinced this band of miscreants that all their lives were missing was the chance to show the man that they wouldn't take being ignored anymore.

He hadn't seen him since he'd been brought to the house earlier that day, but he wondered if he knew how restless his troops were becoming. Hunting zombies on TV wasn't what these guys craved. They wanted real life conflict with the world they'd decided had turned against them.

That Ponytail wanted to make some videos of Persephone, likely with a gun held to her head just for good measure, smacked of something terrorist groups did, but in reality, that's exactly what these guys were. They hadn't had much success yet at being that, but it didn't mean that wasn't what they wanted to be.

He dreaded the moment when one or more of them would pull their heads out of their asses and figure out that sitting around some rundown house in rural Virginia wasn't the way to get the world's attention to your cause. When that happened, he feared they might figure out that holding a hostage is useful, but killing a hostage got you way more press.

Exactly what these assholes wanted.

"Maybe Clayton's got other plans," Nick suggested, unsure how Ponytail would take that idea.

But he seemed resigned to just that and shrugged. "I guess. I don't know. All I know is that this isn't what I wanted to do with my damn time. If we're going to show the world what happens when you forget the most important people in society, then let's fucking show them. We've got a hostage. Let's show them what we can do to her!"

Forcing himself to nod, Nick inwardly recoiled in horror at the thought of what Ponytail and his buddies dreamed of doing to Persephone. Left to their own devices for long enough, he had no doubt they'd kill her, but he had a sick feeling that first they'd take out their resentment on her for everything they mistakenly believed society had done to them.

He couldn't let them do that.

"So we're just supposed to sit around twiddling our thumbs here?" he asked in a tone of phony disgust.

Ponytail nodded. "Yeah, it sucks, doesn't it? Maybe a few of us could make a beer run. There's got to be someplace around that has some. At least being drunk would be better than nothing. Clayton put a stop to smoking, so all we can do now is those fucking pills he lets us have."

"Pills? What kind? Oxy?" Nick asked with an eagerness he didn't have to force. If he was going to be dealing with that kind of shit, he needed to know right then and there.

His question made Ponytail laugh loudly and throw his head back. "I fucking wish! I would kill for Oxy right now. No, Clayton says the pills he got are better, but as far as I can tell, they're nothing, man. They just relax you. Like that's what I want now stuck out here in the hinterlands of wherever the hell this place is."

Nick quietly sighed as relief washed over him. Clayton had probably just given the guys downers to keep them from spinning out of control. Considering all the energy drinks they had consumed just in the time he'd been at the house, he didn't doubt the leader's decision. That combined with the fact that none of them seemed very stable added up to the real possibility that without something to calm them down, they might become uncontrollable at any time.

"So, when is Clayton coming here? He doesn't expect us to just sit around and do nothing for days on end, does he?"

Ponytail shrugged once again and answered, "Who knows? He told Drist he had something else planned for a few days from now, so I guess until then, we're stuck here."

Nick wondered what the leader planned to do as he mumbled, "Some revolution."

"At least we're moving tonight," Ponytail said with a smile that showed off his crooked teeth. "Well, that's what I hear anyway. I just hope we get somewhere closer to where real people live. All I've seen in the past week is cows eating grass and fucking farmers."

So they planned to move to another location that night. That would mean they'd be moving Persephone too. Nick needed to get assigned to that job to make sure they didn't hurt her.

The problem was he had no idea who actually made those decisions. The group of men didn't act like any organization he'd ever infiltrated before. They had no leader present most of the time, and he had no clue who chose who for what job. All he knew was when he showed up Drist had told him he had to feed Persephone, but that was only because he didn't want to do it anymore.

"So, when Clayton isn't around, who's the boss here?" Nick asked as Ponytail walked toward him to leave the room.

He stopped and thought for a moment before he answered, "I don't know. I guess Drist, but that's only because he threatens to kill anyone who pisses him off. But don't worry. Just stay on his good side and you'll be fine."

How he'd be didn't worry him so much as how Persephone would be under the control of that bastard. His need to constantly wave that damn weapon around made him unpredictable, to say the least.

But if cozying up to that madman was the way to make sure she stayed safe, then that's what he had to do. He just hoped Ponytail was right about Drist being the one who would make the decisions.

BY EARLY AFTERNOON, boredom or Clayton's

special pills had overtaken every guy in the house but Drist, so Nick took his chance to get friendly with him and hopefully ensure he could protect Persephone from that point on. He walked outside to find him sitting in the hot midday sun on the back steps that led from the kitchen to the large backyard he guessed went back for at least an acre or so.

As usual, the man had his gun in his hand. Before that moment, Nick hadn't paid much attention to what kind of gun it was. That he pointed it at people all the time had been bad enough.

But now he saw Drist's favorite accessory was a Glock .45. Nothing terribly unique or special, it would certainly do the job when he pulled the trigger.

Nick stared down at him for a moment as he stroked his fingers slowly along the barrel. Jesus, this guy had some love for that gun.

"Hey, man. What's up? Everyone in there is crashed in the middle of the day," he said from the top of the stairs to Drist who sat on the second to last step closest to the sidewalk.

He turned his head and looked up at Nick as he continued to run his fingers over the Glock. "Pussies. Why aren't you in there too?"

"Video games don't do a whole lot for me most days," he said, avoiding the truth that the guys inside were so doped up that they couldn't help but sleep in the middle of the day.

Nodding his head, Drist made a clucking sound with his tongue. "Pussies."

He was a man of few words, and at the moment, he seemed to like that singular word. The idea that he probably had never seen a pussy in his entire life, or if he had, it had been online on some cheap porn site made Nick want to chuckle, but he stifled his desire to laugh at Drist and got down to business.

Taking a seat next to him on the step, he leaned back on his elbows and stretched out his legs. The whole movement was meant to make him look relaxed, but he knew better than to let down his guard as he pretended to stare out at the backyard.

"I hear we get to leave this shithole tonight. Thank God for that, right?"

Drist closed one eye and aimed the gun at some unsuspecting squirrel about fifty yards away. "Hell, yeah. I'll be happy to get the hell out of this farm shit. This man needs the city, for fuck's sake."

"Where are we going?"

The question sounded no more different than the last he asked, but Nick had the sense immediately that Drist heard something in it that bothered him. Turning toward him, he pointed his gun directly at his head and narrowed his eyes in suspicion.

"What's it matter to you? You writing a book?" he asked, his words laced with barely restrained anger.

It took everything in his power to keep calm as he looked down the barrel of Drist's gun aimed squarely between his eyes. His heart beating wildly, Nick shrugged and said casually, "No, man. I just don't have a thing for farm animals, and that's all this place seems to have. Did you see those heifers near the end of the backyard, for Christ's sake? The fucking things just walk around this place like they own it."

His longwinded explanation that diverted into the discussion of his dislike of cows nearby seemed to throw Drist off, and he turned to look around for the cow Nick had mentioned. He likely wanted to shoot the damn thing.

Pointing his gun back toward the yard, he laughed. "I could go for a steak. A big, fat, juicy steak, right?"

Nick forced himself to laugh, sure this guy wasn't playing with a full deck. He had no doubt, though, that if he got the chance, he'd take a shot at the brown and white cow nearly a hundred yards away that now slowly walked away from the backyard.

Crazy fucker. Even animals knew to stay the

fuck away from him.

"It'll be nice to be somewhere we can get a steak and we don't have to kill it ourselves, won't it?" he asked, hoping to get Drist back onto the subject of where they were all moving to that night.

"Yeah. Clayton won't be sending us anywhere good, though. We need to keep moving. A few more nights until he can join us."

"So more houses like this?"

A rabbit about twenty yards away distracted Drist, so he didn't answer for a long moment while he eyed up his shot. When he did, he said, "Yeah. One of Clayton's friends is going to let us use his mother's old house in Winchester. I guess the old broad died a few months ago, and he can't find anyone to buy the place. See, that's what this thing we're doing is all about."

Unsure what the hell he meant, Nick put on his most serious expression and nodded. "I get it, man."

"A guy gets left a perfectly good house and the motherfucker won't sell because fucking McMansions all over the place make the world think that every house has to have twenty bedrooms and fifteen fucking bathrooms. It's ridiculous! That's what this is all about. It's time to take back this world and let guys like Clayton's friend be able to sell his mother's house for a decent profit. I mean, it's got like three bedrooms. What's the fucking problem with that?"

Drist began to unravel there in front of Nick, and he wondered if he should push him for any more details. The guy clearly had a very tenuous grasp on reality to begin with, and whatever the hell he was rambling on about concerning real estate already had upset him.

"I get it, man. Three bedrooms. Hell, I grew up in a two bedroom apartment, and we thought we had it pretty damn nice. We didn't starve, and my father always made sure we had clothes to wear and a roof over our heads. Nowadays, he'd be seen as a loser, but that's bullshit. Total bullshit. He was a good guy, my father."

Nick watched as Drist nodded his head, eagerly agreeing with every word he'd said. In truth, his father had been a Lieutenant Colonel in the Army, and by the time he and his mother had him, they had more than enough money to afford one of those McMansions Drist railed against. He'd grown up in a house five times the size of the house behind them.

The world this crazy fucker hated was pretty much the world Nick had lived in since the day he was born. He wasn't Marshall Gilmore level, but he certainly had never been Drist level.

But he knew how to talk a good game with people like him. They all pretty much had the same story in mind when they thought of themselves. Modest upbringing with decent folks who tried their best to give them a life better than theirs. It was overly romanticized usually, but it helped the Drists of the world think that despite all the good that had been around in the past, now none of it existed anymore because of people like Marshall Gilmore.

The truth was that good they looked back to still existed. They just wanted more. They wanted what the media moguls of the world had but they didn't want to do what it took to get it.

Well, other than kidnap young women and threaten to upend the world order if they didn't get their way.

He didn't give a damn about Drist's distorted belief system or any of their messed up ideas, in truth. He'd seen them all before. All he cared about was finding a way to get Persephone out from under their control before they killed her.

"That's the way of the world these days," Drist said angrily. "People like your old man are losers, while that bitch's father gets to be king of the world. It's wrong, man. All wrong. That's why we have to change it before it gets too out of control and all the good this country has to offer is gone forever."

Good like Drist. Yeah. Right.

"She's never had to worry about the roof over

her head or having enough money to get lunch at school," Nick said with a sneer he added for effect. Pointing toward the room where Persephone sat, he added, "People like her don't get it. They never will."

Before Drist could get himself worked up into a lather, Nick stood up to leave. "I can't talk about this anymore or I'm going to want to go in there and make her pay for all people like her and her father have done. I know Clayton wouldn't want me to do that, though. Whatever else she is, she's going to help us do what needs to be done to change this messed up fucking world."

Drist nodded, grudgingly admitting Nick was right. "Yeah, Clayton would be pissed if we did anything to her. He wants to get more money from her father, so we can't mess up her face."

Pretending to be disappointed he couldn't beat the hell out of a woman, Nick frowned and nodded his head. "I get it. This is a long game. We have to think a few moves ahead. It's like chess."

"Exactly! Chess is exactly what it's like, and those rich bastards aren't going to know what hit them when we start playing," Drist said excitedly and then let out an evil laugh as he pointed his gun at Nick to reinforce his point.

As he walked away, Nick wondered if Drist even knew what chess was. He had a feeling he would be terribly disappointed when he found out it didn't involve guns or zombies or killing anything.

Chapter Six

THE BEDROOM DOOR opened, making a creaking noise that never failed to terrify her, so Persephone quickly turned her head to see who they'd sent in this time so she could brace for what was to come. Eyes wide with fear, she saw Nick again and breathed a sigh of relief. Still unsure what to think about him, she felt reasonably sure he wasn't as horrible as any of the other men.

He walked up beside the chair and crouched down in front of her. Placing his hands on her legs to balance himself, he looked up at her and whispered, "They're going to be moving you tonight. I'm trying to get assigned to be one of the people who goes with you."

She nodded and made a noise to let him know she wanted the gag removed. He reached up and pulled the rag out of her mouth.

"Don't talk loud. We can't afford to have them hear you," he warned.

"Where are they moving me to?" she whispered,

each word painful as her mouth formed the syllables.

"Winchester. I'm going to try to be one of the men who moves you."

Persephone didn't understand why he had to do any of this at all. Why weren't the FBI just handling this like any other kidnapping case?

"Why aren't the police or the FBI involved in this? At the very least, why aren't the state police handling finding me?"

Nick shook his head. "The FBI is involved, but after those farm pictures came out, they probably thought you weren't being held against your will."

A mixture of disgust and disappointment rushed through her brain. Not held against her will? Didn't they look at those pictures? She couldn't have been more obvious with how terrified she was in each and every one. For God's sake, in some she had to force back the tears as that awful man screamed at her to look happy.

"So there's just you trying to save me?" Persephone asked, not sure she wanted to hear the answer to her own question.

Nick lifted himself up so he was eye-level with her. His dark eyes stared into hers and made her feel like what he had to say meant something important to him. At least he seemed to care.

"Your father hired me because this is what I

do. I know you don't trust me, but I'm doing everything I can to make sure you're safe while you're with these men, and I'm going to get you away from here as soon as I can."

"What are they planning to do with me?"

"I don't know yet. They don't seem to either. Most of the guys here are just drifters or unemployed guys who have nothing else to do but a lot of anger about it. They have this belief that the world has given them a raw deal, and their leader has told them the way to remedy that is you."

"Me?" she asked incredulously.

How the hell could she be the way to remedy their unhappy lives?

Nick nodded and rolled his eyes. He didn't seem too convinced by what he had to say. "Yeah. I think the idea was that they'd kidnap you and get money for their cause, but something must have happened because your father already paid them five hundred grand and you're still here."

Suddenly, panic tore through her body. She'd seen enough movies and documentaries to know that once kidnappers got the money they demanded, if they didn't release their prisoner that person wasn't long for this world. Tears welled in her eyes as all hope she'd had of escaping slipped away.

"They're going to kill me, Nick. I know how

this works. They got the money, so now it's just a matter of killing me. Did they send you in here to do it?"

Tears began to roll down her cheeks as her short life flashed in front of her eyes. She'd never married or had children. She'd never even been engaged. All those years she'd spent devoted to becoming a nurse and then getting ahead at the hospital now seemed for nothing. She'd die in this terrible place or the next terrible place they planned to take her to and her life would end as if she meant nothing to the world.

He shook his head and cradled her face in his strong hands. "No! Don't think like that. Persephone, I'm not going to let them kill you. I promise you that. Something must have changed anyway because they demanded another five hundred thousand from your father already. I think they didn't plan on this actually succeeding, so now they just figure they're going to milk it for everything they can. To do that, they need you alive."

"But what if my father already paid that second half a million? What then? They aren't going to keep this going forever," she sobbed.

Nick slowly dragged the pads of his thumbs across the tops of her cheeks to dry her tears and smiled. "I think they're just not very good at this. Most of them spend half the day sleeping because the leader is drugging them to keep them calm. This Clayton guy hasn't been around since I got here, but Drist says he'll be around soon."

"Drist?"

"Short blond hair and way too many tattoos on his face," he explained as his hands slid from her face. "The one who brought me when I first got here. He has a thing with guns. Probably means he's compensating for something."

Persephone couldn't help but smile. There she sat in some rundown house tied to a chair and this man who claimed to be there to help her was making jokes about one of the men outside that room having a tiny penis.

She'd seen enough of Drist's anger to make her want to believe someone had cut off his penis. Even that may have been too good for him, though.

Then it dawned on her that the name Clayton sounded familiar. "What's the leader's name? Clayton what?"

Nick moved his hands away from her face, and suddenly she felt alone, even as he crouched in front of her. Maybe she could trust him. God, she wanted to.

"Berger. My guess is that the FBI has kept him busy these past few days since he doesn't make any secret of the fact that he's the leader of the National Equality Militia," Nick explained.

"But Drist gave me the impression we might see him soon."

Persephone looked up toward the ceiling as the name Clayton Berger settled into her brain. Where had she heard that name before? She had definitely heard his name, but where and why?

Focusing on Nick again, she looked down at him as he sat crouched in front of her and asked, "What does he look like, this Clayton Berger? Have you ever seen him?"

"Just a picture of him online but never in person. He doesn't look like any of these guys, to be honest. He has short brown hair, light eyes, I think. Maybe blue. I'm not sure. He has a look like any regular businessman from what I could tell by the picture I saw. My guess is he's the respectable face of the organization. Why?"

Persephone thought back to a night a few weeks before at the hospital. "Is he tall and thin?"

Nick nodded. "Yeah. Pretty much. Why?"

She knew there had been something strange about that man that night on her last shift of the week. He hadn't seemed in as much pain as he claimed, so the doctor had refused to give him any meds for his supposed pain. He'd seemed more interested in talking to her about what made her choose nursing as a career than actually being in the agony he claimed he was in, and she'd suspected something was wrong with him.

"He came to the hospital where I work last month. He said he'd twisted his ankle and strained his back helping someone move, but he never really looked like he was really in much pain and the x-ray showed his ankle was just fine. I was the nurse who attended him, and all he wanted to do was talk to me about why I chose to become a nurse, if I liked living in the area, and things like that. I'm so stupid. I had a feeling something wasn't right, but I still talked to him for nearly a half hour."

"That was probably Berger getting a feel for you and where you worked since they grabbed you from the hospital, right?"

She nodded, disgusted that she hadn't followed her gut that night. "Yeah. They were waiting for me at my car in the parking garage. That man pretended to be hurt just to get close to me? My father was right. He always told me working at that hospital put me in danger, but I never listened to him. Now my stupidity has cost him a million dollars and might cost me my life."

Nick frowned and stood up in front of her. "No, it won't. Your father may have lost that money, but I'm not going to let them do anything to hurt you. Just remember what I told you. Don't fight them. They've been told to not mess up your face too much, so you should be okay. Hopefully, I can get to be one of the guys who goes with you tonight when we move to the new place in Winchester."

"Will you help me escape then?"

"That's the plan. Okay, I have to go. Just remember. Don't fight them."

He turned to leave, but Persephone hated the idea of being left alone in that room again with the gag stuffed in her mouth. "Wait! Don't go. I'm going out of my mind sitting here for hours alone."

Turning to look at the door, he sighed. "I don't want to risk them getting suspicious of what I'm doing in here."

"Please, stay for just a little while. You want me to trust you, but I don't know anything about you, Nick."

She waited while he decided if he should give in to her pleas and then silently rejoiced when he stepped back to stand in front of her. Persephone still didn't know how much to believe in him, but God, she desperately wanted to.

"There's not much to know about me," he said with a smile that instantly calmed her.

"You say you're not a cop or FBI. Then why would my father hire you to rescue me?" she asked as she sized up the man in front of her.

Tall and strong, she believed he could take any one of the men outside that room. But could he save her from all of them?

Nick lowered his head and said quietly, "I used to be FBI. Since I left, I've done work like this, among other things. Don't worry. You're in good hands. I've been undercover more times than I can remember. Never lost anyone."

As he finished speaking, he winced ever so slightly before smiling. Persephone immediately suspected he wasn't telling her the whole truth, but exactly what part was a lie? Had he not been in the FBI, or had he lost someone on a case? Or even worse, was everything he'd ever said to her a lie and he was just another one of the men holding her hostage for some stupid cause who would kill her at some point?

"Promise?"

The word came out of her mouth before she knew it, and for a moment, she felt foolish. How much could any promises made in a situation like this mean? She wasn't a child. She knew how this would very likely end, with or without this man's help.

Nick crouched down in front of her. With a look of utter sincerity in his eyes, he answered her question. "Persephone, I promise I'm going to get you out of here."

He reached down to pick up the gag and then gently pushed it back into her mouth, looking away as he did so he didn't have to face her while he did it. She understood he had to so they continued to pretend that he was one of the militia and she was still a prisoner.

That didn't mean she liked it, though.

But she wanted to believe with all her heart that Nick, this man who appeared out of nowhere and promised to help her, would be the person he pledged he would be and not just another one of those awful men outside that room who looked at her like everything about who she was filled them with hate.

He touched her tenderly on arm as he moved to leave. "I'll be back in a little while. Don't worry."

A few hours later, two men came into the room where she sat, but Nick wasn't one of them. They forced a burlap sack over her head, thrusting her into darkness, and grabbed her roughly. But she didn't fight them, desperately praying to God that she'd hear Nick's voice at any second telling her everything would be okay. Still gagged and her hands and feet still bound, she was carried out to some kind of vehicle and tossed into the back. Her head slammed off the hard metal floor, and moments later, she faded into blackness.

PERSEPHONE OPENED HER eyes but closed them quickly to avoid the light all around her. Slowly, she lifted her eyelids and tried to focus on her surroundings. Where was she?

The room she now sat in had tan walls and curtains with brown and white geometrical patterns on them. The windows were blacked out like at the other place they'd held her, but this looked more like someone's home and less like just somewhere to hide a hostage. A twin bed sat along the wall in front of her, and above it on the ceiling hung a poster of some sports team's cheerleaders.

She looked down and saw they had tied her to a metal kitchen chair with a plastic red padded seat. Far more comfortable than the last one, it at least gave her some cushion on her behind.

Persephone's head throbbed, although she couldn't remember why it would hurt so much. Had they beat her at some point after they moved her here? She tried to remember the details of how she'd gotten there, but her mind drew a blank.

She remembered the two men throwing her into a vehicle and then nothing. At least nothing until that moment when she opened her eyes.

The urge to cry out came over her, so even though the gag still made it impossible for her to actually say anything clearly, she screamed the best she could and hoped Nick could hear her. Then a thought crossed her mind that terrified her even more than being trapped in that unfamiliar room in that unknown place.

What if Nick wasn't there anymore?

She didn't know why the thought suddenly popped into her head. She barely knew him, and even though she wanted to believe he would help her escape, she couldn't honestly say she could trust him. He'd given her hope, though, and for that, she prayed to God he was still with the militia group.

Her throat hurt, but she screamed until no more sound would come out. Still, no one came. Persephone wondered if the others had found out that Nick had been nice to her. Had they uncovered who he really was? Her mind raced with terrifying ideas of what they'd done to him and what they'd do to her now.

Her only hope to escape gone.

As she thought of him no longer there and then thought of him no longer alive, her emotions spiraled out of control. For two weeks, she'd existed in that chair as an object of hate for those men, threatened and demeaned by every one of them except for Nick. She hadn't believed he could get her away from them so much as wanted to believe he could, but now that meant nothing.

Now she was truly alone again with little hope of ever finding a way out.

Tears rolled down her cheeks as she tried not to think of what would happen next, but it was no use. Her mind raced with scenarios of what they'd do to her. Sobbing, she begged God for deliverance and bargained anything she owned for just one more chance to feel the warmth of the sun on her face again. One more chance to hug her parents and sisters and tell them she loved them.

One more chance to live her life.

She cried until she had nothing left inside anymore. After two weeks of being held hostage, nothing they'd said or done to her had broken her spirit. What broke her was the realization that there was finally no hope left for her to get away.

That hopelessness settled into her heart and mind and took over every inch of her until nothing but sadness filled her. She didn't know why they hadn't killed her yet, but she knew it didn't matter much anymore. They would soon, and when the time came, she'd be alone in whatever room they held her in, nobody there by her side to comfort her as she took her last breath.

Behind her, she heard the twist of the doorknob, but as the bedroom door opened, there was no squeaking noise like before. The person closed the door until it quietly clicked shut, and then she felt footsteps fall on the carpeted floor beneath her. Holding her breath, she waited for the sound of the person's voice to let her know what to expect next.

"Persephone? Are you awake?" a man asked, sounding genuinely interested in her and if she'd awakened yet.

The familiar voice registered in her brain, and she looked up to see Nick staring down at her with concern in his eyes. They hadn't killed him for being kind to her. He was alive!

He hurriedly pulled the rag from her mouth, and even though she didn't know why since she barely knew this person, she couldn't stop herself from crying tears of joy. Nick crouched down in front of her and softly touched his fingertips to her cheeks to dry them.

"I'm sorry I couldn't be here when you woke up. I checked over and over, but you stayed out for a long time. How do you feel?" he asked as he used his sleeve to dry the last of her tears.

How did she feel? She didn't know how to express that. He wouldn't understand how much it meant to her to see his face in that moment when she was sure all hope had vanished.

"My head hurts. I think that's from when they threw me into the truck or the van or whatever they used to get me here."

He lifted himself up and gently ran his hand over the back of her head. "I don't feel any lump, but I guess that's not surprising. You've been out for a long time."

Confused, she wondered what he meant. "How long? I know I don't remember being brought here."

Nick stood up and walked over to the window to pull back the black covering to look outside.

"Three days. They moved you to that house in Winchester that night after we talked, and I thought I could get you out then, but that Clayton guy, the leader, showed up and all hell broke loose. He was pissed that they knocked you out and told them to get you somewhere that didn't look like a crack house. So they moved you here. You've been in this house for two days. I'm guessing they drugged you to keep you out for that long. They had me on security watching the back door, so I could only sneak in every so often to check on you."

She tried to remember anything from all that time, but she drew a blank. Three days of her life gone, in addition to the two weeks they'd taken from her before that.

Covering the window up again, Nick came back to stand in front of her. His face serious, he said, "I need you to remember what I told you, okay? I need you to just trust me. I've got something planned, so when it goes down, you'll have to do as I say for the two of us to get out of here alive."

Persephone had no idea what he had planned, but she'd do as he said. She didn't know if what she felt for him truly could be called trust, but she had to admit she'd never been as happy to see someone like she had when he appeared beside her just a few moments before.

Chapter Seven

Nick carried the bowl of the usual grey slop toward Persephone's room, happy to get away from the militia guys for a little while. Between their need to constantly play that damn video game or talk about it when they weren't playing it and their sudden spikes of rage that usually resulted in one of them pulling a gun on the others, he needed a break from being on edge all the time.

He knew most people wouldn't understand. The idea of spending time with a woman he had to keep tied to a chair didn't seem very healthy, to say the least. Ordinarily, he would have been the first to agree, but these weren't ordinary circumstances.

Just a few more hours and he thought there might be a window of opportunity for them to escape. The group had been told to come to this house on a secluded property at the end of a long country road so nobody would be able to find them. Miles of woods around the place gave them cover.

It also meant he might have a chance to get Persephone away. He just needed one window of opportunity.

He'd watched the men around him for the past three days and noticed they had gotten into the habit of taking the pills their leader gave them every night just before midnight. He suspected they needed them to sleep after days full of energy drinks and fixating on zombie killing. Whatever the reason, he didn't care.

All he cared about was finding that chance to get Persephone out of there alive.

He closed the door behind him and walked toward where she sat in the chair one of them had taken from the kitchen set. Before he did anything else, he removed the cloth from her mouth and tossed it on the bed. He hated that he had to put it back every time he left, but the least he could do was get rid of it as soon as he could.

"Thank you," Persephone said quietly. "I hate that thing more than any other part of all this."

Kneeling in front of her, he smiled. "Even more than when one of the other guys comes in?"

She winced and shook her head. "No. Thankfully, they don't even seem very interested that I'm here anymore, though. Any idea why?"

Her voice sounded so full of hope that he hated that he didn't have better news to tell her.

"Not sure. Your father has paid them twice, and I'd guess they've asked for more money. They also seem more interested in killing zombies than anything else. Well, other than fighting with one another and drinking energy drinks by the case."

Persephone smiled and her eyes lit up. "They sound like a fun group. Maybe I should consider myself lucky that they're the ones who kidnapped me."

Nick scooped up some of the grey gruel out of the bowl and held it up in front of him. "I wouldn't go that far, but I guess it could be worse."

She grimaced at the sight of the runny food dripping off the spoon. "I don't want that," she said, shaking her head.

"Don't make me do the whole airplane thing," he said with a chuckle, trying to be cute.

Her eyes opened wide in surprise. "Don't you dare! You put that spoon anywhere near my mouth, and I swear I won't be the only one wearing it."

Dropping the spoon into the grey muck, Nick accepted she wouldn't be making his task easy. "You know they made me feed you this when you were out, right? I can't let you starve."

"Ugh. You didn't," she said, grimacing. "I think I might be sick."

"It wasn't much. Even out of it, you didn't

want it. But that just means you have to eat now. I'd give you what I had earlier, but it wasn't much better than this stuff."

She craned her neck to look down into the bowl. "What is this?"

As much as he didn't want to admit the truth, he said, "Oatmeal with skim milk."

"And this is supposed to keep me alive?" she asked, looking up at him and then back down at the grey slop in the bowl.

"I guess."

She lifted her head and stared into his eyes with a pleading look that made his chest tighten. "Please don't make me eat this."

Her voice caught on the last word, making him hate the job he had to do. "One bite, Persephone. That's all. Just one spoonful and that's it."

Like a disobedient child, she tightly pressed her lips together and shook her head. "Uh-uh."

He couldn't make her eat, as much as he knew she had to, so he placed the bowl on the floor and sat down in front of her. "Fine. I'm not going to fight you, but if we have the chance to get away from here tonight and you can't run fast enough to not get caught, I can't tell you there will be another chance for us."

Persephone drew her eyebrows in and frowned. "I'll be able to run just fine."

"After sitting in that chair for a week and not eating? You're a little thing, but I might not be able to carry you if we have to be running for a while."

She thought for a minute about what he said and then her shoulders sagged in defeat. "Fine. I'll eat."

He didn't envy her having to ingest that horrible slop, but it had to be done. Lifting a spoonful up to her mouth, he slowly pushed it over her lips. Her expression contorted into one of utter disgust, and she pulled away in a hurry.

"Okay, that's it. I said I'd eat one, and I did," she said, refusing to let the food go down her throat.

Nick couldn't help but smile at her behavior. "It does no good unless you actually swallow it."

"I don't want it to touch the back of my tongue or I'll be forced to really taste it," she said, practically whining.

He didn't know why, but it charmed him more than anything had in a long time. Silently, he promised her that he'd find something better for her to eat for dinner that night. Maybe he could scrounge up a few saltines from the kitchen. Unlike the last couple houses, this one at least seemed to have a few things that resembled food in the cabinets.

She swallowed hard and coughed, shaking her

head. "Oh, that was awful! I think I'd rather starve."

"I'll be back for dinner in a few hours," he said as he stood up to leave. "I'll see if I can find something else for you. We're doing three meals a day now."

"Three? How are they letting that happen?"

"I convinced them that I'm getting pleasure making you eat this even more than before, and they bought it. I think those energy drinks might be making them a little dull in the head."

"Even that Drist guy? I'd think he'd want to restrict my food to once a week."

Nick thought about him, and his stomach clenched. Drist had given him a hard time about feeding her more often until he reminded him about feeding her like a dog. He just hoped he didn't follow him in one of these times and actually demand to see her eat like that.

But Persephone didn't need to know anything about any of that.

"He's too preoccupied with his gun and all the reasons he has to be angry to care much about your eating habits," Nick lied. "I'll be back in a little while. I promise."

"Wait! Do you have to go so soon?" she asked as he moved to place the gag back in her mouth.

Going was the last thing he wanted to do. The only happiness he enjoyed occurred when he spent time with her. He'd even thought to himself more than once that when he got her away from these people that he'd miss her. It made no sense. He knew that. He knew practically nothing about her. But from the moment he saw her beautiful deep brown eyes in that picture as he sat in her father's office, he could only think of one thing.

Protecting her.

If he didn't watch himself, he'd fall in love with her before he even kissed her for the first time. And yes, he'd thought of that already too. That made no sense either, considering the mess the two of them found themselves in, but there it was.

And now that she stared up at him with those beautiful eyes that made him want to take her into his arms and never let her go, he had to stuff that fucking rag back in her mouth and walk out of that room pretending like it didn't make him feel like shit.

"I can't stay too long in here. I don't want to make them suspicious," he said, avoiding her gaze as the lame words left his mouth.

"Oh, okay," she said sadly.

She lifted her chin and opened her mouth slightly for him to do what he had to. The rag in his hand felt like a ten pound weight he couldn't lift, but he had to do it.

He didn't have a fucking choice.

Without saying another word, he pushed it into her mouth and fastened it behind her head before leaving the room. He wanted to look back. He wanted to stay there so she wouldn't have to sit tied to that chair with a goddamned rag stuffed in her mouth.

But he didn't have a choice.

DRIST WALKED UP behind him and leaned over Nick's shoulder as he made Persephone's dinner of vegetable soup. Every inch of his body froze as the man's breath skittered over the skin on the back of his neck. He knew that gun of his was somewhere near him, making him all the more terrifying as he stared down at the bowl of soup.

"What the fuck is that?"

Nick turned his head and saw up close the black tattoos that covered the side of Drist's face. Christ, he was ugly!

"Soup."

"Why is she getting that?"

His heart slamming into his chest, Nick tried to stay calm and minimize the change in her meals. Stirring the liquid, he shrugged.

"I thought maybe we should make sure she doesn't starve to death. That wouldn't be a good thing. I figured Clayton would be pissed if that happened, so I thought I'd try some soup. It's nothing I'd eat. All those fucking lima beans make me sick. It should be called bean soup."

Drist narrowed his eyes and looked into the bowl once more. "Still too good for the likes of her."

And just to punctuate his point, he spit into the soup before walking away.

Nick quickly scooped it out of the bowl and rinsed off the spoon before heading into where she waited for him. As he closed the door, he felt something push against it and turned to see Drist coming in behind him.

"What the fuck, man? You almost made me spill this shit all over me," Nick snapped as Drist slammed the door behind him.

Persephone turned her head to look at him in horror as she realized who had joined him to feed her. Although Drist probably loved to see her looking so frightened, he hoped she knew that he wouldn't let him hurt her.

"I wanted to come in and see how you handle her. Bitches like her need to be taught a lesson."

"Don't worry. I know how handle women like her," Nick said with as much anger as he could muster.

He quickly put the bowl of soup down on a nightstand next to the bed and turned around to make sure that crazy bastard hadn't drawn his gun on Persephone already. He hadn't, but the sneer on his face didn't make Nick feel any better about the situation.

"She's nothing. It's time she learned that lesson," Drist said, practically spitting each word out of his mouth.

Stepping forward to defuse what he knew could quickly become a very bad situation, Nick nodded like he agreed with what the crazy asshole said. "Don't worry. She'll know once I'm done with her."

And then he raised his hand as if he planned to hit her across the face. Persephone recoiled in horror, turning her head to avoid the sting of a slap against her cheek.

"See? I've already got her trained pretty good. Give me another day or two and she'll be eating out of my hand."

Drist seemed pleased by the threat, like holding her hostage wasn't enough to make her feel like nothing. "Good. Make her see who's boss."

He laughed like some evil hyena and turned around to head back out. Happy to see him gone, Nick picked up the bowl and approached Persephone again. She refused to look at him, though, instead staring off toward the other side of the room, even when he removed the gag from her mouth.

Crouching down in front of her, he took his

usual place to feed her and whispered, "I'm sorry about that. I didn't think he'd leave if I didn't show him that I hated you too. I wouldn't have hit you. You know that, right?"

She didn't respond, but he saw her frown deepen as her face remained turned away from him. As much as he knew he had to put on that act for that asshole, he couldn't help but feel guilty for frightening her. Hoping to show her she could trust him, he untied her ankles to give her some relief, at least for a few minutes.

But still she refused to look at him.

Touching her on her arm, he said, "I need you to eat some of this soup. Come on. It's not that grey crap anymore."

Persephone turned her head and looked down wide-eyed into the bowl he held in his hands. "Soup? Is that really something other than that terrible grey stuff? They let you give me soup?" she asked, looking up at him.

He smiled, happy to see her dark eyes filled with something other than fear. "I told them it wouldn't be a good thing for you to starve to death. I guess they bought it."

A look of worry came over her face, and she quietly said, "I thought you were going to hit me."

Her words felt like a punch to his gut. Shaking his head, he lifted the spoonful of vegetable soup to her lips. "I wouldn't do that. Well, I don't want to. But if it meant the difference between me doing it and someone like Drist there doing it, I would just to make sure he didn't touch you."

She swallowed the soup and nodded. "That tastes so good. I don't think I've ever loved vegetable soup as much as I do right now."

"Even the lima beans?" he asked with a chuckle as he fed her another spoonful of soup.

Nodding, she smiled as she let the soup go down her throat. "Yeah. Even the carrots too."

Nick knew Drist might return at any minute, so he needed to make sure Persephone understood whatever he did in front of those men was what he had to do to protect her in the long run. As he continued to feed her, he tried to explain what might happen.

"I need you to remember that I'm trying to make sure we get away from here, hopefully tonight. Drist and those guys seem on edge this afternoon, so something might be about to happen."

Persephone swallowed hard and frowned again. "Something? Like what?"

He didn't know what could happen, but a restless group of malcontents holed up in a house never meant anything good. He hoped they'd get lost in another night of zombie hunting and even

Drist might find another few hours of amusement in that damn gun of his.

"I don't know. Most of them out there are bored, so that could spell trouble. I just need you to trust me. No matter what happens, no matter what I have to do, I just need you to trust me, okay?"

She nodded and took the spoon into her mouth before swallowing more soup. "Okay. Like you might hit me?"

Jesus, he hated this. The last thing he wanted to do was hit her, but if that meant none of them did, then he'd do it or whatever else to keep their hands off her.

He stared into her eyes and hoped she understood what he meant. "Whatever I have to do, I'm doing it to protect you. Just remember that."

Persephone stretched her legs and ankles. "Did you really never lose anyone while you were at the FBI?" she asked in a voice full of fear.

Lying to her would be the best thing, but he didn't want to. Whatever they were there in that horrible situation, at least she should know that he was truthful with her, even when it hurt him to be.

Nick shook his head. "No. I lost one person, and the next day, I left the FBI."

Her eyes wide, she asked, "Someone you were

helping when you went undercover?"

He swallowed hard and took a deep breath before admitting the truth to her. "No. An informant who died because of me. After that, I couldn't do my job without regretting all that happened."

A noise at the door startled them, and Nick looked up to see Drist and the rest of the group coming into the room. Their restlessness had finally exploded into something more dangerous.

All at once, Nick knew their time was up. Whatever happened now, he had to make sure they didn't hurt her.

Persephone's body tensed up in terror, and she looked like she was about to cry. Nick brushed his hand against her leg as he stood to deal with them in an effort to signal that he wouldn't let anyone hurt her now that the time had come.

"What's this? A fucking convention?" he asked angrily, pissed he now had to deal with the whole group of these guys in with him.

"Drist said you had her under control, so we wanted to see," Ponytail said as he leered at Persephone like a hungry man seeing his first meal in days.

Fear coiled in Nick that what he and the rest of them were hungry for wasn't food but her. "So you all thought you should come in so we can all stand around like fucking idiots while I feed this bitch? Zombies get too boring for you guys?"

Most of them laughed at his joke, but Ponytail couldn't take his eyes off her and reached out to grab her between the legs. Persephone snapped her head around and clicked her teeth together to bite him on the arm but missed, angering him. He jammed his hand into her crotch again, harder this time, and she reacted by kicking her leg out at him.

That's all it took to make the rest of them lose it, and they began screaming for him to fuck her and show her who was boss. Nick quickly saw his control of the situation begin to unravel, and fearing they might gang rape her if he didn't do something, he threw the bowl of soup toward the nightstand and pushed hard against Ponytail's chest to get him away from her.

"After all I've had to take from this bitch, I should be the one who gets the right to have her. You haven't been stuck in here every goddamned day fucking feeding her like some kind of motherfucking servant she's probably used to."

Out of the corner of his eye, he saw the look of pure terror wash over her face as the reality of what they planned to do settled in among the room.

What he would do.

"Well, let's go!" one of them near the door

barked.

They all began to yell their lust for him to fuck her. She looked at Nick and began begging him not to do it, but her pleas were drowned out by their voices.

"Like I want to fuck her in front of you all," he said with all the bravado he could find inside.

All five of them seemed confused by his reluctance to have sex with Persephone with them watching. For a moment, he thought he'd gotten out of it, but Ponytail wasn't having any of that.

Stepping toward her, he grinned. "Well, if you won't fuck her, I'm going to."

Nick's heartbeat pounded in his ears as he realized he couldn't back out. No amount of bravado or shit talk would distract them from what they wanted. They'd consumed too many energy drinks and played too much of that zombie video game and now they needed something to sate their need for excitement.

And if he didn't do it, one of them would and he couldn't risk her getting hurt by one of these guys so filled with rage and dying to direct it at her in any way possible.

"She's mine," he said in a voice full of possession. "If you want to watch like a bunch of fucking ladies in waiting, whatever. But she's mine for all I've had to take from this bitch."

Before Ponytail or any of them decided to

challenge him on that claim, Nick walked over to where Persephone sat and began untying the ropes holding her firm to the chair. She looked at him in stunned silence, her eyes pleading with him not to go through with this.

He roughly lifted her from the chair and turned to toss her on the bed to the cheers of the men around him. She landed hard, and before she could move to fight him, he leaned down next to her face as he pinned her hands above her head.

In a voice he hoped they couldn't hear, he whispered in her ear, "Don't look anywhere but in my eyes. I promise I won't let them hurt you."

As he leaned back to unzip his jeans, he saw the look of betrayal in her eyes. It nearly broke him, but if he didn't do this, one of them would. There was no other choice.

"Do her!" one of them screamed, and the others repeated his command over and over.

Nick roughly stuck his hand into her green scrubs and yanked them off her legs. She cried out, begging him to stop, but he couldn't. Tearing her panties off, he laid on top of her and thrust into her body, never taking his eyes off her face.

Her sobs filled his ears, drowning out the cheers from the men around them. Lifting his body off hers so he didn't crush her, he continued to thrust into her. She stared up at him, just as he'd told her, and he slid his hand around her neck to feel something in the act other than the sickening feeling of betrayal.

Never before in his life had he seen such pain in someone's eyes and all because of him. With every thrust into her body, he knew that would never leave him for the rest of his life. That it shouldn't leave him.

Finally, she closed her eyes, and he sensed every word he'd said to her fading away, replaced by hatred and distrust.

Chapter Eight

In the darkness, Persephone sat tied to that kitchen chair wishing she could curl up in a ball and die. She'd dared to let herself believe that Nick would protect her, but he'd shown her no one could protect her anymore.

Her stomach roiled, the bile rising in her throat as her mind replayed every moment of those men cheering him on like he was doing something worthy of applause. Hate surged through her for those pigs and him because he was no different from them.

She wanted to hide her shame, but she couldn't. Instead, she had to sit there in that room alone as the memory of what had been done to her refused to go away. Powerless and terrified, she waited for the moment when the next one would come in and take their turn with her.

Persephone closed her eyes and hung her head. How could he have done that to her? How could he have promised to protect her in one breath and then forced himself into her in the next?

She didn't want to cry anymore. She had no more tears anyway. They'd all been used up with every time she cried out for him to stop.

For the first time in days, she felt utterly hopeless. Everything she'd built up in her mind—all the possibilities Nick offered, all the chances she believed would come because he was on her side—all of that disintegrated the moment he gave in to the cheers from those animals hours before.

Now the reality of what would happen to her couldn't be denied. They'd keep her alive as long as her father continued to pay them or until they got as much as they needed, and then they'd kill her. In the meantime, they'd use her as a sex slave, torturing her with rape to punish her for whatever crimes they'd convinced themselves she'd committed because of who she was.

A tiny flame of resistance still existed somewhere deep in her mind telling her to keep working to loosen the ropes around her wrists and keep trying to wriggle out of the rope keeping her in that chair. It quietly whispered that she was stronger than anything any of them—even Nick—could do to her.

She wanted to believe that voice. She wanted to remember how it felt to be truly strong again. But after what he'd done, she didn't know if she had enough strength inside her to continue fighting.

All she knew now was if she did escape from this hell, it would be because of herself and no one else.

Opening her eyes, she looked around in the darkness and couldn't help feel despondent. She didn't know how to do this. She wasn't strong enough or smart enough or brave enough.

Nothing in her life had prepared her for this. Nothing growing up, not college, not even her job as an ER nurse. She'd seen the ugliest sides of humanity, or at least she thought she had. Bodies shot up by bullets fired in hate between people. Limbs severed by car accidents caused by drunks. Overdoses by children who wanted to playact being adults in a world that didn't protect them.

And none of it had made her ready to be tied to this chair for days on end and attacked by men who hated her for merely having the name Gilmore and the money that went with it.

The sound of someone twisting the doorknob behind her made her eyes open wide in terror. She sat frozen to the spot as her heartbeat raced in anticipation of who would enter.

Silently, she prayed to God to give her the strength to withstand whatever they forced on her. Please let me get through this. Please stay with me and watch over me as these men do their evil.

The door opened and the person walked in silently, stopping behind her. They bent down next to the side of her head so she could feel their breath on the shell of her ear. It felt hot and forced, like they were panting.

Then the person touched where the rope held her wrists behind her and began moving it around. Were they loosening her restraints? And if they were, why? To rape her again?

She turned her head to look, but the man had disappeared behind her. Was she losing her mind?

"What are you doing? Who are you?" she asked in a muffled voice through the gag still stuffed into her mouth, desperate to hear another voice other than hers to prove she wasn't going mad.

He tore the gag out and quickly covered her mouth with his hand so she couldn't speak. In her ear, a familiar voice said, "Don't talk. When I undo these ropes, I'm going to need you to stand up."

Nick quickly untied the ropes around her wrists and around her body and ankles holding her to the chair. She tried to stand, but her legs buckled underneath her and she fell to the floor with a thud.

In the darkness, she saw his silhouette standing over her, barely visible because of a tiny glint of light coming from a window at the back of the house. He said nothing but scooped her up into his arms and began walking toward that light.

Persephone didn't want to have to be carried by him. She didn't want him to touch her. She wanted nothing from him ever again. But she couldn't even stand on her own yet, so for the time being, she remained silent, never forgetting how it felt when he betrayed her in favor of those monsters.

He set her on her feet so she could lean against the wall before he slowly lifted the black covering and opened the window to the outside. The first breath of fresh air she inhaled into her lungs nearly made her cry. Freedom smelled every bit as good as she'd always heard it did. She'd just never realized how sweet simple air smelled.

Leaning out the window, she saw a ladder that travelled down the back of the house to the ground. She turned to look at him, worried how she'd get down two floors on her own.

"I don't know if I can do this," she admitted, hating what that meant.

He nodded. "I'm going to have to carry you. I need to put you over my shoulder, okay?"

She waited for him to lift her up, but he simply stood there staring at her like now he needed her consent to touch her. Confused, she shook her head at his hypocrisy.

"What? So now you're going to ask me to let you do something to me? This you need permission for?"

Nick hung his head and quietly answered, "I just have to put you on my shoulder, Persephone."

The way he said that made it seem like he was the injured party. Like her question made him feel bad. She wanted to pound her fists into his chest and scream at the top of her lungs how much she hated him for what he did, but that moment wasn't the time.

"Fine. Do whatever you need to do," she said in a clipped tone that barely disguised her hate for him.

He looked up and for a second she thought she saw a look of hurt in his eyes. No. He didn't get to feel hurt by the way she treated him. He didn't have the right to feel anything but shame.

The same shame she felt from what he'd done.

"I'm going to carry you down the ladder, but I need you to make sure you don't hit the side of the house and make noise. I'll try to be careful, but I just wanted you to know ahead of time."

The kindness in his voice sounded very much like how he'd always sounded when he spoke to her, but now she hated it as much as she hated him. She hated how it revealed a gentleness in him she'd believed in.

How it reminded her that she'd put all her faith in him.

Nick gently lifted her over his left shoulder and eased himself out, lowering his body so she wouldn't hit her head on the bottom of the window. The warm night air covered her, all at once making her feel refreshed and excited. They just needed to get down this ladder and away from this house and she'd be free again.

She clung to him for her very life, even though his very touch reminded her of what he'd done just a few hours before. It created a sense of confusion inside her she didn't know what to do with.

For his part, whatever he thought about what he'd done to her that night seemed to be something he could push aside whenever he needed to. He took each step slowly, methodically descending to the ground as he held her tightly to him.

When he finally took that last step into the grass, she held her breath, terrified one of the men would be waiting for them. Looking around, she frantically searched the backyard for anyone who would try to stop them but saw no one.

Nick walked toward the gate at the end of the backyard, careful to stay in the shadows the trees on the side of the property offered. He said nothing as he carried her through the night toward the freedom he'd promised to give her again.

As much as she wished she could focus on that, all Persephone could think about was how she'd stared up into his eyes as he thrust into her and saw nothing in them that said what he was doing bothered him in the least. She suspected he'd claim he had to do that to her so no one else would, but that didn't make it better for her.

And the fact that he'd rescued her and now carried her to freedom in the dark of night away from those monsters didn't either.

He pushed the metal gate in the chain link fence open, but it squeaked so loud he stopped before walking through. Turning around to look at the house, he waited a moment before turning back and hurrying out of the yard.

They were just a few yards from the house, but they were free.

"Put me down. I think I can walk," Persephone said as he walked into the woods near the house.

Nick stopped and set her gently on the ground. Her legs wobbled a little, but she wanted to be free of having to depend on him to get away.

"Come on. We need to get further into the woods before they realize we're gone," he said pointing into the darkness of the forest.

But she didn't want to be trapped in there with him.

"I'm fine on my own now. I'll be sure to tell my father you did your job so you can get your money," she said angrily as she looked around for which way to go now that she was free.

He grabbed her arm and held it tightly as he shook his head. "No, you're not. You barely can walk after being in that chair all those days. I promised your father I'd get you home, and that's what I'm going to do, even if I have to carry you all the way there myself."

Persephone tried to yank her arm from his hold, but he was too strong. Her emotions on edge after all that had happened, she lashed out at him and pounded her fist into his chest.

"After what you did, I never want to be anywhere near you again! Let me go!"

Clamping his hand over her mouth, he scolded her. "They're going to hear you if you keep yelling like that. You don't have much choice in the matter, so you're going to have to trust me and let me pick you up."

He lifted his hand, and she said, "Like I trusted you before and you…"

The words got trapped in her throat, and she stood there as her emotions began to unravel inside her. Nick winced, like her words bothered him, but he said nothing before simply picking her up in his arms and walking off with her into the woods.

The last thing Persephone saw of that house they'd escaped from was a light turning on in the upstairs room where she'd been held. Tapping Nick on the shoulder, she pointed toward the house.

"They know I'm gone."

He stopped and looked back, and she felt his entire body stiffen. But if he was as afraid as she was, he didn't show it as he began walking faster into the darkness, saying nothing to her.

PERSEPHONE DIDN'T KNOW how long they traveled into the woods, but even being carried began to make her legs ache like they had for every minute she'd been tied up to a chair. She knew he had the harder job carrying her and had to believe he needed to rest.

"Can we stop for a minute? You have to be tired, right?"

He shook his head and continued walking. "Not yet."

"My legs hurt. I just want to stretch them for a minute."

Turning to look at her, his face no more than a few inches from hers, he narrowed his eyes in anger. "I said not yet. There's a cabin up here about a mile away."

He trudged up a hill, bouncing her up and down with every step and making her back ache. "I just want to stretch. I've been stuck in that seat for two weeks."

Still, her pleas fell on deaf ears. Nick shook his head and continued walking toward the cabin he claimed existed somewhere out in these woods. The man had a lot of nerve refusing her even this tiny request after everything that had happened.

"I'm not going to run away, if that's what you think."

Nick turned to look at her and smiled. "That's exactly what I think since you told me you wanted to go off on your own back there. I can't let you do that."

Frustrated, she said, "You know, you're no better than those animals back there. No better."

He didn't respond to her taunt, but she knew it bothered him because he grimaced briefly after the words left her mouth. She didn't regret them, though, and not because he wouldn't stop to let her stretch her legs.

They continued in silence until he made a sound like a grunt of relief and she turned her head to see that cabin he promised they'd stop at. But even then, he didn't speak to her. He simply kept walking.

"How long are we staying here?" Persephone

asked.

"Just long enough to get rested and then we'll leave. I want to have you home by tomorrow night."

The way he said that sounded like he didn't want to have to deal with her or the job of rescuing her anymore. She didn't know why that bothered her, but it did. She was the aggrieved person, not him, Goddamnit.

"Good. I want to get home and see my family again," she said, not even trying to mask the hurt his dismissiveness made her feel.

Nick pushed open the back door to the cabin and walked into the darkness inside. Persephone could make out basic shapes and saw a couch on the far wall of the room.

"Put me down over there."

He did as she ordered and set her down as gently as he had picked her up back at the house. It felt so good to stretch her body, especially her legs. As he searched for some light, she closed her eyes and let herself truly relax for the first time since those two men grabbed her in the hospital parking garage. The couch may have been old with a spring that poked into her lower back, but it felt like heaven to her after the past couple weeks.

She breathed in the musty odor of the cabin that smelled nothing as sweet as that first breath of air she inhaled hours before but she didn't care how dirty or dilapidated this place was. She was free.

How she'd escaped from her kidnappers weighed heavily on her mind as she lay there in the darkness. If it hadn't been for Nick, she would still be back at that horrible house tied to a chair with a gag in her mouth. That she had him to thank for the gift of her freedom made hating him confusing and difficult. She wanted to hate him. She had every right to hate him.

But at the same time she owed her life to him.

From the other room she heard a noise and turned to see him walk toward her holding a lantern that lit his way. His expression showed how tired he was from carrying her all the way there, and a tiny lick of guilt pricked at Persephone for every time she silently swore to hate him that day.

"I found this in the kitchen. It's not a lot of light, but it's better that we don't have lights on all over the place just in case they come looking for us here."

She noted how he said us and not you. It wasn't just her in this but them together. As much as she wanted to believe he was no better than those monsters who'd held her hostage, she knew that wasn't the truth.

But that didn't make what he'd done any

easier to forgive.

"Okay."

He gave her a half-hearted smile and pointed toward the kitchen. "There's not much in there to eat, but I did find some crackers and some canned food. I can get you something, if you want."

She shook her head. Eating was the last thing she wanted to do, even though she would have thought that she'd want to gorge on food once she was free. In fact, just the thought of food made her feel queasy.

"No, thanks. I just want to rest here and stretch my legs."

His frown made her think her answer disappointed him, but she couldn't imagine why. Taking a seat in a chair across from her, he sat down with a groan.

"That sounds like a good idea. We'll get going again in a little while."

She waited for him to say something else—what she wanted him to say she didn't know—but he simply set the lantern down on the table between them and leaned back in the chair to close his eyes. Persephone watched him as he sat perfectly still and wondered if he fell asleep after a few minutes of not moving at all.

As she looked at him, she also couldn't help but wonder what he felt about what he'd done. She knew no matter how much she wanted to say he was a monster like those men who kidnapped her that wasn't true. He had rescued her like he promised, and she believed his actions proved he wasn't an animal like them.

But how did he feel about what had happened? Did it bother him that for those few minutes he had been as cruel to her as each of those horrible men had been?

She watched him from across the room as his chest rose and lowered over and over and wondered what thoughts ran through his mind at that moment. Was what he did replaying on a loop in his head at it had with her while she sat tied to that chair and left alone in the dark?

Or was it all just part of the job he agreed to do for her father to find her and bring her home?

Could he rationalize what happened back in that house that easily, or would he have to talk about what he did at some point?

Closing her eyes, she tried to push away the memory of him thrusting into her while all those monsters cheered for him to fuck her harder, but she couldn't. Over and over, her mind replayed the scene until all she felt was rage.

As tears rolled down her cheeks, she turned away from him so he wouldn't see her crying. She didn't want to cry anymore. She didn't want to hate anymore.

She just wanted to go home.

Chapter Nine

I N A FLASH, he opened his eyes and looked across the room to the couch to make sure Persephone still lay there. He hadn't planned on falling asleep, especially since he had a feeling she'd take the first chance she could to get away from him and chasing her around the dark woods wasn't anything he wanted to do that night.

Not that he could blame her for never wanting to be near him again.

He watched her all curled up sleeping soundly and hoped to God the memory of what happened back at that house didn't haunt her even in her dreams. He couldn't do anything about that now, as much as he wished he could turn back time and change what he did.

She'd never forgive him. He knew that for sure. How could she? He couldn't, so he didn't see how she could.

Taking a deep breath, he let it out slowly while he worked to force his brain from replaying that one horrible act over and over. He'd done some terrible things in his life that he'd have to live with until the day he died. He accepted that as part of the job he chose to do. He could have just become a run-of-the-mill private eye or something benign like that after leaving the bureau. Spend all his time finding lost relatives for money and being bored out of his mind.

At least then he wouldn't have regrets. Well, other than throwing his life away in exchange for being safe.

But he chose to become a hired gun because he needed the rush going undercover had always given him. He liked the danger. Hell, he loved it. He fed off it. Infiltrating some group and pretending to be one of them for the greater good gave him the adrenaline rush he craved and the ability to do good that made his conscience feel right at the end of the day.

That made up for that mistake he made back in his bureau days.

So what if he had to act in ways other people found immoral? He got the job done, and when it was all said and done, that's all that counted.

He'd always been able to tell himself that when questions popped up in his mind about the things he'd done all in the name of the job. This was different, though.

Persephone made it different.

Never before had he cared enough for a client

to do what he did. He knew how fucked up that sounded. Even he had a hard time thinking that, but it was the truth he couldn't escape.

He did what he had to so the rest of those monsters didn't do the same to her.

Not that an excuse like that would ever be one she'd accept. He knew that. It didn't change what he believed, though.

Over on the couch, she stretched her legs and made a mewing sound that hit him like a knife to his heart. Was she having a nightmare about what he did to her? Is that why she whimpered like she was in pain?

Fuck. He needed to get her back home so she could forget him and return to her life of whatever media mogul's daughters and heiresses to one of the world's biggest fortunes did with their days and nights. Her father would insist she have security round the clock, which was good because who knew when another group like the National Equality Militia bastards would try again. And next time that group might be worse and not let her live after taking the money.

She needed protection. He suspected that she needed a lot more after what she'd been through. Hopefully, some day she'd find this all just a bad memory she overcame. He hoped so. He didn't believe for a second that she'd ever accept that he did what he did to protect her, but at least maybe she could come to forget the harsher edges of the memory.

Even if he never would.

Persephone rolled over and faced him. Still asleep, she curled herself into a ball and tucked her hands under her chin. She looked content somehow after all she'd been through. That could be true, right? He wanted to think it could be, even if he had to delude himself into believing it.

Whatever the truth was, the sooner he got her back home, the sooner he wouldn't have to think about this entire job anymore. Like every other time in his life when he'd done something he knew people wouldn't understand, he'd push it down deep inside and do everything he had to so he didn't think about it.

He looked over at Persephone and felt a twinge of sadness. Forgetting what he did would mean he had to forget her. In the short time they'd been thrown together, she'd somehow found a way past his defenses and into the part of him he let almost nobody see. He didn't know how she did it either. One minute she was just a client he needed to rescue, and the next minute he was trying to figure out what excuse he could give those bastards why he needed to be in that room with her.

A tiny voice whispered what he already suspected for days. He was entirely too close to this case.

To her.

It had happened to him once before. Tanya. He'd let his guard down and fallen in love with her, and what had she gotten for that? A few months of happiness with him before some fuck killed her when he found out she was his informant. It was as bad as if he'd taken her life himself.

He'd made a mistake, and that mistake had gotten her killed. No matter how long he lived, he'd never forgive himself for that. He'd known all the reasons why that was one of the worst things anyone on the job could do, and he still he let himself fall in love.

Falling in love with someone you were trying to save was no different. He knew that. What two people went through when the world was raining shit down on their heads didn't equal love. Nick didn't know what it equaled.

Other than the fucking risk of both of them dying because his feelings clouded his judgment. He couldn't let that happen again.

What he felt for Persephone couldn't last. Wouldn't last. And that was before he had to prove to those militia fucks that he was one of them by taking her in that room as they cheered him on.

His chest ached at the very thought of it. As if

someone had his heart in a vice, he couldn't breathe every time he thought about what he'd done.

It didn't matter that he had to. It didn't matter that he did it so he could lay claim to her so none of those monsters would. None of that mattered.

All that mattered was how she'd believed in him up until that moment when he looked into her eyes and slowly pushed his hips forward...

Cringing, he shook his head to force himself to stop thinking about it. He fucking did what he did to protect her. It didn't make him the goddamned man of the year, but it accomplished what he needed it to. They didn't touch her and at least he knew she was safe.

"I'm hungry."

The sound of her voice roused him from his horrible mental torture, and he stood up to head to the kitchen. Anything to escape being there with her and his thoughts.

"I'll get you some of those crackers I found before."

He hurried out of the room and began to rummage through cabinets as he pretended to look for food. Anything to not have to go back in there to face her so soon. His stomach churned, not from hunger but from disgust. He had no idea how he'd spend the next few hours with her until this case ended.

The sound of footsteps made him turn toward the doorway, and he saw her standing there looking up at him with a confused expression, like she couldn't imagine what would take so long to find some damn crackers. He closed the cabinet in front of him and walked over to the pantry where he'd found the food earlier.

"I don't know how old they are, and they're only saltines," he said in a low voice, unsure what to fill the empty space with but needing to say something.

Turning around, his gaze met hers. He wasn't sure, but he thought he saw hatred even as she patiently waited for him to hand her the box of crackers. It made him stop short and nearly recoil, but he pushed his guilt down for at least that moment.

"Here you go," he said, handing her the food before he walked past her out into the main room of the cabin.

He hoped she'd stay in the kitchen to eat. Actually, what he really hoped she'd do would be avoid him until they were forced to be together once again in a few hours. He couldn't afford his emotions getting the best of him, but if she kept looking up at him with those big brown eyes so filled with anger at him, that's exactly what would happen.

All he needed to do was get her home safely. Once he did that, they could continue on with their separate lives like before all this happened.

Before he sat back down in the chair, he checked the windows in the room to make sure they didn't have any uninvited guests. Staring out into the darkness, he scanned the area around the cabin but saw nothing moving and no one out there.

They knew by now he'd taken her. They'd be looking for the two of them—her to take back to the house and him to kill for betraying them. The single gun he had wouldn't be much if they all came at them at once, but he had a feeling most of the militia group didn't know much about guns other than how to use them in video games to kill those damn zombies.

Drist, on the other hand, knew all too well how to use a weapon. While he may have wielded it mostly to scare the hell out of those unfortunate enough to be around him, Nick knew better than to fool himself into thinking the guy didn't have experience with guns. He and Persephone would probably be okay if one of the others found them, but if Drist caught up with them, he'd be more than happy to take a shot at him. He might even shoot her. The guy didn't seem as committed to the militia's cause or Persephone's kidnapping as he was to just wanting to hurt people.

Nick took a deep breath as the thought of that fuck hurting Persephone settled into his brain. No way. He may not have been able to make up for what he did to her, but he could make damn sure none of those sons of bitches got to her while he was around.

"What are you looking at?"

He tugged the drapes closed and shook his head. "Nothing. Just wanted to make sure we haven't been followed here."

She lifted a saltine to her mouth and took a bite. "Oh. Okay. There's no one out there then?"

"No. Don't worry. I'm not going to let them take you again. We'll leave here in a little while and as soon as we reach somewhere my phone works, I'll call your father so he can send someone to get you. You'll be home soon. I promise."

Persephone sighed and took another bite of cracker. "Don't make promises you can't keep, Nick."

He opened his mouth to assure her he'd get her home soon, but then he realized that wasn't what she was doubting. Nothing he could say would ever convince her he did what he did to fulfill the promise he made to her to never let those men hurt her. He knew that, so there was no point in trying.

Better to say nothing.

They stood there in the middle of that room

staring at one another like each one waited for the other to speak. Her eyes fixed on him, she looked like she knew exactly what she wanted to hear come from his mouth. He didn't know what that was, though, so he said nothing.

In fact, if it was up to him, they could both remain silent until the moment he returned her to her family. At least then there would be no chance either of them would say something they'd regret.

He'd had enough of regrets on this case.

Now all he wanted was to be done with it.

"Do you need to stand guard near the window all night? Won't you get tired?" she asked in sweet voice.

Brushing off what sounded almost like concern for him since that couldn't possibly be what lay under her words, he said, "I slept a little before. I'm fine. You should lay down again. Might as well take advantage of the time to stretch your legs while you can."

She bent over and looked down at her legs before looking up at him. "I'm fine to walk now. I'm not sure I can run much, though, but I think if someone was chasing us, the adrenaline would kick in and I'd be able to run anywhere I had to."

Nick stood next to the window and forced a smile as he pointed at the couch. "Well, take it easy for a while. We'll leave in a little while."

Taking his cue, she sat back down and

continued to eat her crackers. When he didn't move after a minute or so, she asked, "Would you like to sit down with me? I thought maybe we could talk."

Every muscle in his body stiffened like lead. Talk? What the hell were they going to talk about? Even if the hate seemed to have left her eyes, he suspected none of it had actually disappeared. He didn't begrudge her feeling that toward him, but the last thing he wanted to do was sit down and listen to her tell him how much she hated him for what he'd done.

"I want to keep watch," he said quietly, hoping that would put her off wanting them to talk.

She didn't say anything for a while and instead continued to eat the saltines until there were none left in the box. Placing it on the table, she stared at him for so long that he felt like her gaze was burning a hole in the side of his face.

But he didn't turn to look at her or ask if she needed anything. He knew what she needed and he didn't want any part of it.

"I'd really like to talk. If you won't come over here, can I come over there?" she asked using that sweet voice again.

What could he do? He couldn't avoid her while they were stuck in that tiny cabin, but talking wasn't going to change what he did.

As if reading his mind, she said, "I just wanted to talk. We don't have to if it bothers you, but it would mean a lot to me if we could."

That made it even worse. Now if he refused to talk to her, it would be like he was unwilling to give her the one thing she'd ever asked from him.

Reluctantly, he walked over to the couch and sat down on the opposite end from her. A spring poked the back of his leg, but he had no intention of moving any closer to her while they talked. Being this close already made him uncomfortable.

Persephone cleared her throat and said in a tiny voice, "I just wanted to thank you for getting me out of there."

Looking down at his legs, he shrugged. "I was just doing my job. Your father paid me to get you away from those bastards, so I did."

He didn't have to see her face to know his answer had disappointed her. Of course it did. When you thanked someone for doing something for you, being told it didn't mean much wasn't exactly what you hoped to hear in return.

"Well, even though it was your job, I still wanted to say thank you. You put yourself in harm's way the entire time you stayed with those men just to get me out, and that's something no one can put a price on. Not even my father."

"I did what I had to, Persephone. That's all it was."

Never before had he spoken truer words to anyone in his life. He didn't know if she understood the true meaning of what he said, but he hoped someday she'd think back to this moment and remember that he confessed the real reason why he did what he did.

Lost in his own thoughts, he didn't realize she'd moved over on the couch to sit right next to him. Placing her hand on his forearm, she said, "I know you did. I wanted to hate you for it—in fact, I did ever since it happened. But now that I've gotten some sleep and had some food other than that grey stuff, I don't. I'm not sure what to think about it, though, other than being ashamed."

For the first time since he sat down on the couch, he looked over at her and saw her head hung. He hated hearing she felt shame over what he'd done. She didn't deserve that on top of everything else she'd gone through.

"Don't be. It was nothing more than if I pretended to want to hit you. It was a show for their benefit to make them see they shouldn't touch you or they'd have me to deal with."

She lifted her head, and her beautiful mouth turned down into a frown. "I'm not sure that makes it any better, to be honest. But thanks for trying."

He hadn't meant to make it seem like having

sex with someone was on the same level as someone pretending to want to hurt them. His mind raced with some way to explain what he really meant, but nothing came to him. Christ, how did anyone explain forcing themselves on someone to protect them?

"I know it sounds wrong, but I did it to make sure they knew I'd claimed you. It's how people like them think. If you belonged to me, then they would think twice about touching you. I just wanted to keep you safe from them."

She turned her head to look at him with confusion in her eyes. "Belong to you?"

He knew how ridiculous it sounded to say someone belonged to another person. He didn't think like that, but that group of militia assholes did. They saw no use for women other than as sex toys for them to play with every so often when they weren't fucking around with guns or trying to kill zombies.

"I just wanted to make sure they understood that if they touched you, they'd have to deal with me. If they thought you were mine, they likely would keep their hands off you. It's who they are. They have the mentality of animals, so I staked my claim."

It all sounded so clinical and at the same time barbaric, so he stopped for a moment and then said, "I'm sorry I did that. I didn't have a choice, but I didn't mean to hurt you like that."

Fighting back tears, she nodded. "Well, in medicine, you sometimes have to remove a part of the body to save the person. Maybe if we look at it like that we won't both feel bad about it someday."

Thinking about forcing himself on her as like amputation probably wasn't going to help him feel any better about it now or in the future, but if that worked for her, he could handle it. As long as she knew that he had done it to protect her and not hurt her.

He smiled and nodded, but just then a noise outside drew his attention. Jumping to his feet, he stepped in front of her. "Stay behind me."

As his heart raced, she stood up and they backed up away from the window. Nick pulled his gun and prepared to shoot whoever was out there. He'd protected Persephone before, and he'd do it again.

And he didn't give a damn how many of them he had to kill.

Chapter Ten

THE SOUND OF someone jiggling the handle on the back door of the cabin made Persephone's blood run cold. She'd foolishly convinced herself that she and Nick had gotten away from those crazy militia guys and this cabin was a safe place for them.

Even after all she'd been through, hope still insisted on making a fool of her. So much for wishful thinking.

Nick pressed the back of his body against hers and whispered, "If someone comes through that door, don't worry. I'm not going to let them get to you."

Terrified, she pressed her hands to his back and felt the muscles in his shoulders coiled tightly together as he waited to see if whoever was outside would try to come in. For the first time, she saw him holding a gun. Part of her couldn't help be thankful he had one, but another part of her worried if the person outside came in shooting, they'd all end up dead.

"Please don't get killed, Nick," she whispered behind him.

He didn't respond. A second later, the door opened and she saw a figure she recognized standing there. The light from the lantern barely showed his face, but she'd know those horrible tattoos anywhere.

"You should have run farther, man. It took nothing to find you," Drist said in his usual terrifying tone that made her feel sick to her stomach.

"Turn around and leave," Nick said flatly. "There's nothing for you here."

Drist closed the door behind him and waved his gun in front of his face. "I'll tell you what. I don't have to kill you, Nick. I get it. You fucked her and now you want to protect her. I don't get why you give a fuck about this one, but I guess I get it. But she's got to come back. We need her. You know that."

Nick stuck his arm behind him to squeeze Persephone's hand. "You can't have her. Go now or you'll end up with a bullet in your head."

For a moment, Drist looked surprised to find a gun in Nick's hand. Then his eyes narrowed and he shook his head. "I had a feeling you were too good to be true. You're not one of us, are you? Her daddy sent you in to get her, didn't he?"

Persephone clutched onto Nick's shirt and felt

his body expand beneath it as he took a deep breath. "Leave now or you'll be leaving in a body bag. Whichever, but you can't have her."

Drist took a single step into the cabin and aimed at Nick standing in front of her. Instinctively, she closed her eyes tightly as the sound of the gun going off was met with another from the gun in Nick's hand.

She didn't know how long she stood there cowering behind him, but when she opened her eyes, he was still there standing in front of her, protecting her. Had he been shot? Had Drist been shot?

"Nick! What happened?" she cried out as she clutched tightly onto his shirt, afraid to let go.

Slowly, he turned around to look at her. His eyes focused on her face for a long moment, and then he said flatly, "We need to get out of here."

Her attention moved from him to the body of one of the men who'd held her hostage for the past two weeks. Drist lay on the floor just inside the back door in a pool of blood.

"Are we just going to leave him there? He might still be alive," she said, fighting every instinct she had as a nurse to attend to his injuries.

"He's not alive, Persephone."

"How do you know? If he's still alive, we have to find him help. No matter how evil he is, we can't leave him if he can be saved," she said as she watched Drist's chest for any sign he still lived.

"He can't be saved. I shot to kill," Nick said quietly without a hint of emotion in his voice.

Rushing around him, she ran over to where Drist lay. Crouching down, she pressed her fingers to his throat to check for a pulse. She felt nothing. The amount of blood and brain splatter on the door behind him told her Nick had been right.

"We have to go, Persephone. Leave him there."

Torn between not caring at all that one of her captors lay dead next to her and her duty as a nurse to care for people who were hurt, she remained next to Drist. That Nick had killed him didn't bother her, but leaving him there to rot felt wrong.

"We can't just leave him there. Can't we bury him, at least?" she asked, walking over to where Nick stood staring at her with a look of confusion on his face.

"Sure. You hang out here while I did a grave. It shouldn't take me longer than an hour or two. Meanwhile, we can put the light in the window to let the rest of those bastards know you're here for the taking."

Sarcasm dripped off every word, but it didn't seem right just leaving Drist's dead body there on the floor. "We shouldn't leave him like that."

For a long moment, she watched as what she said filtered through his brain, but then something snapped inside him. He stormed over to where she stood and grabbed her by the shoulders.

"This guy would have happily killed me and then taken you back to that house so he and his buddies could take turns raping you. You want us to take precious time out of escaping from those guys, who are likely very close by, to respect his dead body?" he barked at her.

His use of the world raping stunned her. It came out of his mouth with such rage. That single word that held such a loaded meaning between them made her emotions spin out of control, and she couldn't stop herself from crying suddenly.

Hanging her head, she sobbed as he took her by the arm and led her out of the cabin into the darkness outside. After everything that had happened, the way he said that single word broke her.

Nick held her wrist as he began running, and she struggled to keep up with him. A pain in her side stabbed at her with every step she took, but he didn't slow down so she couldn't either.

Persephone didn't know if they were running away from Drist's dead body, the truth of what happened between them, or the other men of the militia group that might be close by. All she knew was Nick seemed possessed by the devil himself to get away from that cabin as fast as possible.

Gasping for breath and barely able to run another yard, she begged him to stop. "I can't go anymore. We need to slow down."

He looked back at her and shook his head. "We can't. I can't let them find you."

She tore her hand from his hold and stopped dead, unable to go another step. "No! I can't keep up with you!"

Nick stopped running. "If they find you, they're going to take you back there. I won't let that happen."

Looking around, she saw no one in the woods with them. "They're not here. Maybe Drist came alone. I don't know, but I can't keep running like that."

He hung his head and avoided her gaze. "I can't let them find you. I can't."

"I know, but they're not going to. You're right here. They aren't going to get me," she said as she slowly walked toward him to take his hand.

They stood there together, their hands joined, and she knew what he was running from. But no matter how far they ran or how fast, the truth of what he did would always be there. She could forgive him for what he did, but he couldn't forgive himself.

✦ ✦ ✦

THE BLACK TOWN car pulled up to the curb, and before it even fully stopped, her father opened the passenger side door and stepped out. Opening his arms wide, he smiled at Persephone.

"I'm so happy to see you again, honey."

She ran to him, happier than he could ever imagine to be back in his arms. He hugged her tightly to him like he might not ever let her go again.

"Thank you for sending Nick to rescue me, Dad," she said as she pressed her cheek to his chest and heard his heart racing just like hers was. "I wouldn't be here with you if it wasn't for him."

Above her, he said, "Thank for bringing my daughter back to me. I don't know how I'll ever repay you for this. Money just isn't enough for what you've given back to me."

"You don't have to thank me. I did the job you hired me to do, Mr. Gilmore," Nick said in a strangely distant voice that made her look back at him.

He avoided meeting her gaze and focused on her father instead. "She's been through a rough time. I'd suggest putting a security guard or two on her and your other daughters for a while. The National Equality Militia is still out there."

"About that. They brought in Clayton Berger

a couple hours ago after the FBI raided a house where most of the group was staying. His men didn't take long at all to roll over on him and tell the whole story about what they did for the past few weeks. You two must have gotten out just before the raid."

Persephone watched Nick wince as her father explained the men in the house had told everything about the kidnapping. She knew what he was thinking.

Would he ever be able to forgive himself for what he did?

"I want to go home and take a long bath, Dad."

Her father smiled and pressed a kiss to the top of her head. "Of course. Mr. Hanson and I can talk when we get to the house."

He returned to his seat next to his driver, leaving Persephone and Nick to sit in the back seat of the town car. Even though her father rarely said much at all since he tended to be a quiet man in his private life, he seemed to have words to spare now as he carried on a conversation with Nick while the car rolled toward the Gilmore estate. Persephone wanted a chance to talk to the man who saved her life, but her father never came up for air, so the opportunity never presented itself.

When the car pulled up in front of the house,

she reluctantly got out without saying what she wanted to and Nick exited the car to go into the house with her father. Her mother and sisters ran out to greet her, full of hugs and tears on her return, so she was forced to watch him walk away before she could pull him aside to tell him what was on her mind.

He never looked back once.

A voice next to her asked, "Persephone, did you hear me? Are you okay?"

She turned her attention to her mother. She'd seen her a few nights before the kidnapping, but now as she looked at her, she saw the past few weeks had changed her. Still stunning with shoulder length warm brown hair and the same brown eyes as all three of her daughters, now worry seemed permanently etched into her normally delicate features.

Wishing she could erase that from her beautiful face, Persephone forced a smile for her benefit. "I'm fine, Mom. I swear."

Cradling her face, her mother searched her eyes for the truth, not believing Persephone was truly okay. "Are you sure? I thought I'd never see you again, honey. Thank God you're back safe with us. Your father told me to trust in the man he hired. He said he'd bring you back to us. I wanted to believe him, but I was so worried."

Her sisters sobbed in happiness to see her safe

and sound again, but all Persephone could think about was how she would get a chance to see Nick before he walked out of her life forever. She couldn't let him do that before she could speak to him once more.

AFTER RUSHING THROUGH a shower to wash away every remnant of her captivity, she hurried down to her father's office at the back of the house and waited outside for Nick to come out. She heard voices inside, so she hoped she hadn't missed him. Pressing her ear to the door, she strained to hear the conversation, but all she heard sounded like her father talking on the phone to someone.

Finally, after waiting fifteen minutes, the door opened and Nick walked out into the hallway. Surprised, he immediately stepped back away from her.

"What are you doing here, Persephone?"

She couldn't help but smile. "My family lives here, Nick."

"I meant here outside your father's office when I came out."

She took a step toward him and stopped. "I wanted to talk to you before you leave."

He didn't say anything, but his expression told her he wasn't sure he wanted to hear what she needed to tell him. Before the past couple weeks, that may have stopped her, but now she needed to speak her mind.

Reaching out, she took his hand in hers and pulled him toward the back door to the garden. "Come with me so we can talk in private."

He reluctantly agreed and walked out with her without saying another word. She guided him to the gazebo at the far end of the gardens and sat down just as the sun began to rise. Nick remained standing and folded his arms across his chest.

Confused by his standoffish behavior, she asked, "Is something wrong? Did I do something that makes you think I deserve such coldness?"

He shook his head and softened his body language, but still he remained standing. "No. Nothing's wrong."

But everything about him seemed wrong now. Gone was the kindness he showed her all those times he came into that room to feed her. Gone was the concern for her. Gone was everything in him that had given her hope.

"Then why won't you even sit down next to me again?" she asked, hurt from the way he insisted on staying away from her.

"Your father's driver is supposed to be taking me home. I'm sure he's waiting for me right now."

God, his words sounded so hollow now! Why

was he acting like this?

Her hands shook as she tried to find the words she wanted to say. "I just wanted to say thank you for everything you did to protect me. I told my father this and I meant it. You're the reason I'm home alive again. Whatever he paid you isn't enough."

Instead of accepting her thanks or saying anything kind like he had all those times when she sat there tied to that chair in front of him, he merely nodded but remained silent. Persephone didn't understand why he was treating her like this—like they didn't know one another any better than two strangers.

Anger and hurt rose inside her until she couldn't stand it anymore. Jumping up, she walked across the gazebo and stopped in front of him. "Why are you acting like I don't even deserve a kind word now? What happened to the man who was back there at that house with me? Where did he go?"

She watched as he narrowed his eyes and stared down at her, wincing as she finished speaking. All she wanted were the answers to those questions. She deserved those answers.

"Persephone, you're home safe now. Don't fight your father when he tells you he wants you to have security. You're strong. You'll forget everything that happened someday. Have a good life."

He moved to leave, but she grabbed his arm to stop him. That's all he had to say?

"Have a good life? You have nothing else to say to me? You were the only lifeline I had day after day. I came to depend on you, and you give me some throwaway Hallmark card greeting after all of that?"

Sheepishly, he looked down at where her hand sat on his arm and said, "I don't know what you want me to say."

"You killed a man to protect me, Nick. How can you act like I'm some meaningless stranger to you now? Why won't you even look at me?"

He lifted his head and she saw such pain in his eyes that her breath caught in her chest. "I can't do this, Persephone. Have a good life and stay safe."

With that, he pulled his arm from her hold and walked out of the gazebo and out of her life. She watched him leave and didn't understand what had happened. She'd told him she understood why he did what he did.

Why wasn't that enough?

Chapter Eleven

NICK TOSSED AND turned for the third night in a row, still unable to forget the look of sadness on Persephone's face as he walked away from her without saying what he knew she wanted to hear. He didn't know which was worse, the look of utter betrayal in her eyes as he held her down on that bed or the look of hurt when he couldn't tell her how he truly felt about her before walking away from that gazebo and out of her life forever.

This was how it had to be. That's what he told himself every time he thought of her and how much he wished she could be right there in his arms at that moment. Better for her to think he never cared, that he was just some guy who felt nothing when he acted like those animals he pretended to be with. That would make it easier for her to get past all that happened.

At least he hoped that would be the case.

In truth, he had no idea. He believed Persephone was strong. Stronger than any woman he'd ever met. But strength might not be enough to overcome all she'd gone through.

Her father would get her the finest doctors in the world to help her. He'd spend his money to do whatever it took to make her life normal again. Not that Nick blamed him for that. As far as billionaires went, Marshall Gilmore turned out to be one of the better ones he'd ever heard of.

He'd expected his meeting with him to involve her father hurriedly stuffing a check into his hand and then giving him a quick goodbye before he was escorted out of the enormous house like some kind of second-class citizen. It didn't happen that way, though.

Instead, Marshall Gilmore sat next to him in one of the two chairs in front of his massive mahogany desk and thanked him for saving his daughter. In his eyes, Nick saw genuine appreciation for what he'd done. And he'd shown that appreciation even more when he gave him an additional hundred thousand for his work.

It made him feel like a fraud sitting there listening to a father thanking him profusely for saving his daughter's life when he knew what he'd done to her would stay with her forever. He tried to convince himself that in the big scheme of things, all things being equal, freedom was a hell of a lot better than still being held hostage, no matter what it took to get that freedom.

But all things weren't equal. He knew that. The fact that a billionaire media mogul paid him four hundred grand to save his daughter like he was reaching into his pocket for change showed Nick the idea of equality had nothing to do with this situation.

And any mental bargaining he did to excuse taking her like he did showed in harsh detail that nothing about what they went through could be considered equal. Nick wasn't equal to Persephone or her family, and his actions that day in that bedroom weren't equal to her freedom.

All he could hope for was she would go on to live a happy life married to some wealthy guy who could give her enough love and enough things to make her forget everything of those weeks of her life.

In that hope resided one of the most painful parts of all of this for him, though. He wanted to see Persephone happy, but it made his chest feel like someone stuck a knife in him every time he thought of her happy with anyone else. Even some guy her father chose for her because of his net worth and ability to give her anything her heart desired.

He shook his head and pulled the pillow over his face. Whatever he thought he felt for Persephone as he fed her each day meant nothing compared to the chance she now had to be happy and safe. He couldn't give her that. Well, maybe he could give her happiness, but not the kind she deserved.

The memory of her smile as he tried to convince her to eat some of that grey shit they forced him to feed her for the first few days made that wish of having her there in his arms come rushing back into his mind again. In the middle of the worst thing that had ever happened to her, she smiled at him and made something horrible sweet for just a few minutes. She deserved that sweetness for the rest of her life.

She wanted him to show her that he'd cared when he thrust into her as those monsters cheered him on. He knew that as he stood looking down at her in the gazebo a few nights before. He could have told her the truth. He could have said he knew it was crazy, but he'd begun to feel something real for her in those days he had to pretend to be one of the militia. He could have told her going into that room to see her each time was one of the few bright spots in an otherwise ugly thing he so desperately wanted to forget.

He wanted to tell her all those things. He wanted her to know that even though it seemed impossible, he had somehow ignored all the people around them when he pushed into her body. He'd told her to focus on his eyes because he hoped she'd see the truth in them.

That in the short time he was around her, he'd fallen in love with her.

Nick tossed the pillow across the bed and watched it roll off onto the floor. Turning to look at his phone, he saw the time.

3:46.

Three nights of not being able to sleep because his mind refused to forget what it needed to.

Three nights of regrets piling up and making him hate himself even more than he thought he could.

Her father had all but given him the green light to stay in her life in that last meeting in his office. "Persephone clearly thinks highly of you, Mr. Hanson. You two have been through something most people have no experience with. I can understand if you stay in touch. I know my daughter. You saved her life. Don't be surprised if you now have a fan for the rest of yours. She's that kind of loyal person."

He'd sat there in that brown leather chair staring back at him and hating himself for the real truth of what they'd been through. No matter what the reason, he'd done something even he couldn't think about without being overcome with self-loathing.

And if Marshall Gilmore knew, he'd likely have him killed and no one could blame him.

Yet Persephone, the very person he'd wronged so terribly, showed nothing of hate or anger toward him that night when he walked out of her father's office feeling guiltier than he'd ever felt before. The hate he thought would forever be reflected in her eyes had disappeared, replaced by something else that made him want to think they could be in each other's life like Marshall Gilmore had suggested.

But as soon as that hope cropped up inside him, he snuffed it out. He had to. For as much as she may have been able to see past that one act to believe in him, he couldn't do the same for himself.

No matter how much he wanted to so he could say she was still in his life.

Grabbing the remote off the nightstand, he flipped through the channels to find something to take his mind off her. A horror flick could work. C-SPAN might bore him to sleep. That could work too.

Anything to let him forget her for at least a little while.

Channel after channel flew by with nothing worth stopping for, but then as he clicked through the news channels he saw her right there on his TV. She looked fresh and clean and as beautiful as she had that night in the garden. Her long brown hair hung in loose waves around her face, softening the sharpness of cheekbones models would kill for. Her deep brown eyes looked different now, framed with makeup to show them off, but they still gave anyone who took the time to notice the impression that when she looked at them, she saw them through a filter that made her think they were kinder than they actually were. More a reflection of her gentle nature than theirs, those eyes could make a man get lost in them.

He'd seen her only in green scrubs for all that time she was a hostage and then a light blue t-shirt and jeans that last night they spoke. Now she wore a black long sleeve dress and a gold necklace with a diamond pendant hanging from it, and in her ears sat diamond studs. Her look screamed class and money and made Nick think how poorly he fit into that world of hers after all.

Turning up the volume, he listened to her speak and knew all of the exterior so carefully created to give her that look of the upper class wasn't who she truly was inside. No matter how much money they spent on that dress or the jewelry, when she spoke, the kindness that transcended class and wealth came through loud and clear.

The TV interviewer leaned in toward Persephone and said in a soft voice, "Miss Gilmore, tell us how you got through your ordeal.

What helped you to make it through everything you had to deal with?"

Nick listened intently. One of the few conditions he'd given Marshall Gilmore before he walked out of his office was that there must be no mention of his name or his part in bringing Persephone home. Her father had assured him his name would never be released to anyone who asked, even the police and the FBI. His job required that he be nameless as much as possible.

She smiled and looked at the woman before looking directly into the camera. "I believe I had a guardian angel who watched over me. He protected me, and for that, I can never thank him enough."

Sure she'd give a vague comment about her belief in God and strength like all people who'd been through something horrible said in interviews, he sat back against his pillow and sighed as he listened but didn't hear anything about religion or spirituality. She simply repeated that she'd had a guardian angel who saved her. Nobody had ever referred to him as a guardian angel. He'd been called all sorts of names, but never that.

"What are your plans now, Miss Gilmore? What do you want to do most of all now that you're back home?"

Nick knew the interviewer probably expected

her to say she wanted a double cheeseburger with bacon or something equally as frivolous. That was usually the kind of thing victims of traumatic experiences said in interviews like this. It made them appear to be normal and ready to return to the regular world. He suspected Persephone had been told to give an answer like that but slightly more refined. She was, after all, the daughter of a billionaire. People could excuse her wanting something a bit more than a fast food meal on her return to daily life.

He watched as Persephone smiled and nodded before answering, "I have a lot I want to accomplish, but first on my list of things to do is finding a way to make sure no woman ever has to go through what I went through, Angie."

The newscaster looked genuinely surprised by that answer and attempted to ask a follow up question to get more details, but Persephone refused to give any. All she'd say was she planned to devote her life to that one goal of ensuring no woman would ever have to experience what she had.

Nick didn't know what she meant exactly, but he knew if anyone could achieve that, she could.

Holding the remote in his hand, his thumb hovered over the button to change the channel as he stared at Persephone Gilmore for a few seconds more before the screen faded to black and a commercial for some kind of home gym began. She had looked as incredible as he knew she would. Now all she had to do was find that wealthy man to marry and her life would be set.

That he hated the very idea of that happening made him wonder if he was as much a monster as any of those militia fucks. Or maybe he was just selfish.

Either way, he felt certain it made him the last person in the world Persephone should be with.

No matter how much he wished the opposite was true.

NEARLY A WEEK of no sleep made Nick feel like a bus had hit him and then backed over his head just for good measure. If he kept going like he was, he'd end up in some mental hospital clutching his knees and rocking back and forth as he recited the alphabet backwards.

He hadn't had a sip of alcohol in years, but as this bout of insomnia inched into a second week, he wondered if the moratorium he'd forced on himself a year after leaving the bureau now seemed a little too strident for his current circumstances. Back then, he'd let himself become a drunken mess after Tanya's death and walking away from the only life he'd known for so long. He lost himself in the bottom of a glass for months on end, draining not only bottle after bottle of whatever liquor he could find but his bank account as well.

Now he knew better, though. He didn't need to drink to drown his misery. That misery would be there when he got sober again anyway, so if he went back to drinking now, it would only be so he could sleep.

Rationalizing all this as he dressed to head out to get a few bottles, he threw on a shirt and pants and slipped his feet into a pair of shoes before opening the front door to his apartment to see Persephone standing there with her hand raised ready to knock. How she found where he lived ran through his mind, although that question seemed pretty dumb since her father could have told her or she could have just hired someone to find out for her. It wasn't like he lived off the grid.

He just preferred to remain unknown. It suited who he was.

"Nick, I was just going to knock on your door," she said with a beautiful smile.

But all he could think of was how she shouldn't be there. She should have been anywhere else but there with him.

"I'm just leaving," he said brusquely. "I have to go."

She put her hands out and pressed lightly

against his chest as she looked up at him with those dark eyes that threatened to swallow him up. "Please don't push me away. I need to speak to you."

The feel of her touching him made his head swim with guilt and need, never a good combination of emotions. He felt his feet move backwards into the apartment, and Persephone followed him, closing the door behind her.

Swiveling her head left and right, she looked around his home and smiled again. "This is so very much you, Nick. Very few decorations and very functional."

At that moment, nothing in him seemed to be functioning right. He couldn't be there with her. Why she didn't understand that he couldn't fathom, but he didn't know the words to explain it to her either.

"Persephone, you shouldn't be here. You should be home. I didn't see anyone in the hallway. Why aren't you letting your father have security watch you?"

Her smile faded. "I'm not a child, Nick. I'm guessing you're not that much older than I am."

"It's for your own safety. You should let him do that."

Nick didn't know why they were having this argument. He had no right to tell her what to do with her life. That he hated the idea of her being hurt again so much it made him want to kill someone meant nothing.

Taking a step toward him, she touched his hand gently before squeezing it. "I need to talk to you."

"About what?" he asked, sure he didn't want to hear the answer.

"I've been doing a lot of thinking since what happened. I have some ideas about what I want to do now, but I'm not sure how to implement them," she said, grimacing as she admitted that truth.

He didn't know what she meant, but he saw it clearly bothered her that she hadn't been able to start working on these ideas yet. Some part of him wanted to help, but he knew better. What happened between them would always get in the way of anything they did together.

No matter what it was or how much he wanted to be around her to help with anything she could need.

"I don't know what I could do to help," he lied, hating how dismissive the words sounded as they came out of his mouth.

Persephone let go of his hand and hung her head. "What have I done to you to deserve being treated like this, Nick? Will you just tell me so I can fix it?"

He stared down at her as she stood there

completely dejected and felt the self-loathing wash over him again. She hadn't done a damn thing to deserve this from him. If anything, he should be working day and night to earn her forgiveness for what he did.

And even knowing all of that, he still couldn't see how anything but pushing her away would be good for her.

"I don't know what you mean. You don't have to fix anything. This is just who I am," he said, mixing his lies with that single truth in the middle.

She lifted her head, and he saw she didn't believe him. "No, it's not. You were good and kind to me all those times you came into that room where they kept me tied up. You made me smile. Where is that man who became my lifeline? I would have given up if it wasn't for him. Where is he in this functional world you live in?"

Suddenly, watching her protest against his lies became too much for even him to stand. He didn't want to be the person who pushed her away, even if a voice in his head screamed that what he'd done would forever haunt them.

Taking hold of her hand, he squeezed it gently and smiled. "I don't know how you've forgiven me, but I'd give anything to know how to do it."

Her eyes filled with tears. "How to forgive me? What have I done? Tell me and I promise I'll make it up to you, Nick."

He shook his head, unable to understand how she couldn't admit what he knew. "You have nothing to make up to me. It's me who owes you. I can't forget what I did, and no matter how many times I justify it, I can't forgive myself."

Chapter Twelve

"THERE'S NOTHING TO forgive. You saved my life. Nothing else matters," Persephone said, suddenly realizing the depth of his guilt.

Knowing why Nick had been so cold to her the week before made her wonder how much he'd tortured himself over that one act. Out of everything he'd done to save her, he'd focused on that one moment in time until it pushed out all the good he'd done.

He dropped his hold on her hand and backed away, just as he had practically every time he'd been close to her since that nightmare ended for them. Turning his back on her, he said in a low voice, "You should leave now."

"I don't want to leave, Nick. I want to stay and tell you that you don't have to be forgiven for anything. You don't."

But he just shook his head. She needed to say something more to get through to him or he'd never forgive himself. She couldn't live with that.

Touching his back, she felt him exhale and

watched his shoulders drop.

"Please listen to me. You shouldn't feel guilty about anything you did. Without you, I'd still be at that house, tied up to that kitchen chair with a gag in my mouth. Because of you, Nick, I'm free from that. I know what you can't forgive yourself for doing, but I already forgave you."

"You shouldn't have," he said in a low voice laced with anger.

She walked around to stand in front of him, but still he wouldn't look at her. "Please, Nick. You're the only person on earth who knows what I went through. I have no one else who shares that with me."

Nothing she said worked. He simply winced like her words caused him pain. She needed to get through to him, so she swallowed hard and bared her soul to the only person who might understand.

"I go to this therapist nearly every day since I got back. It's the only time I get away from everyone's eyes on me, so it's sort of a break. Is that messed up or what? The people who love me watch me like a hawk, and that bothers me. I know why they do, but I'm not going to just disappear one day, you know?"

She watched for any response from him, but still he just avoided meeting her gaze. So she continued her confession.

"So I go to the therapist and she listens to me talk about what I went through. She's helpful because I need to talk about it but there's no one around who truly knows what happened, so I tell her. She doesn't say much, Dr. Wilson. Sometimes she tries to explain why I feel the way I do, but mostly she just sits and listens. I tell her about how at the age of twenty-eight I'm suddenly afraid of the dark. How terrified I get in the darkness now. Things like that. She says that will go away. I don't know, though."

Nick pressed his lips together, as if he needed to stop some words from falling out of his mouth. Persephone desperately wanted to hear those words, but still he remained silent.

Turning away, she told him what she said to the doctor about the man who saved her. "I talk to Dr. Wilson about you. My father told me I couldn't tell anyone your name, so I call you my guardian angel. I told her how you made me hope when I didn't have any reason to hope I'd ever get away from those men. I told her how it got to the point that the only happiness I could find in my day was when you came to see me."

Behind her, Nick exhaled a loud sigh. She couldn't bear to see his face as she continued because she couldn't handle his rejection again. For a moment, she hesitated telling him what else she told her therapist, but something inside her spurred her on, so she continued, her voice shaky from fear.

"I told her what we did and why it happened. I told her that I hated you when it was happening, but now I see that it was you trying to protect me from those monsters. She claims I'm suffering from Stockholm syndrome or something like it because I care about you, but I think she's wrong. It's not that simple, even though she makes it seem like it is."

She stopped talking for a moment before she admitted the raw truth she couldn't escape. "I've stopped telling her how I feel when it comes to you because I don't want to hear her say what I feel for you isn't real or good. It just hurts too much to think that you and she think the same thing."

The room around her fell completely silent, except for the sound of her heartbeat slamming in her ears. Never before in her life had she been so terrified of saying anything, and now that Nick seemed to have no response to her confession, every fear she'd had that the therapist was right threatened to overwhelm her.

"Persephone…"

Oh, God! She knew the sound of pity when she heard it. She'd had a lifetime's worth of it since she returned home, and she hated it.

Spinning around, she saw Nick staring down

at her. She looked into his eyes and there it was. Pity. He didn't care about her.

"Don't look at me like that! I'm not some pathetic thing who deserves pity! I know what I feel, so don't try to tell me I don't feel that way about you. I don't need your permission or anyone's permission to care about you, although at this moment, I think I must be as crazy as that therapist of mine thinks I am to feel anything for you."

He said nothing, and as she waited in vain for even a single word, all the humiliation she'd dreaded washed over her. The therapist had been right. He didn't care for her like she cared for him.

Pushing past him, she hurried toward the door as the room began to close in around her. As she reached for the doorknob, Nick touched her softly on the shoulder, making all the need for him come rushing back.

"Persephone…"

"Please stop saying my name if you have nothing else to say."

She stared at the grey front door in front of her waiting for him to continue, to put her out of her misery or to let her go. Either one would be better than being stuck in this emotional limbo he held her in.

"Don't go."

Had he asked her not to leave? She questioned the ability of her ears to hear two simple words, sure they'd been mistaken.

Slowly, she turned around to see him looking down at her with anticipation in his eyes. Unsure of everything but how much she missed seeing kindness from him, she swallowed hard and repeated what he'd said to her.

"Don't go?"

He shook his head and smiled. "No. Don't."

She waited for him to say something else, but he fell silent. Unlike that night at the gazebo, though, he didn't push her away with his silence. She saw the man who had protected her all those times in that room at that horrible place once again standing in front of her.

"I don't want to. I want to stay here. With you."

Her voice trembled as she admitted why she'd come there. Yes, she did want his help with her plans for the future, but even more, she wanted him to be a part of her future.

She wanted him.

"Tell me you didn't believe what that therapist said about me, Persephone," he said in a low voice.

Full of anguish, the words sounded like someone was pulling each one from his throat. She knew the pain he felt at the thought that what existed between them wasn't real. She'd felt it every time Dr. Wilson practically dismissed her feelings as this syndrome or that complex.

She bit her lip before telling him what he needed to know. "I don't care what anyone else thinks. They don't know what we went through. I can't explain why I feel the way I do, but it isn't in spite of what you did. I need you to know that."

He bowed his head when she referred to the single event that threatened to push them apart. "I can't forgive myself, so I can't understand how you could forgive me."

Reaching out, she took his hand in hers and brought it to her mouth in a kiss, loving the feel of his strong knuckles against her lips. The strength she'd relied on all those days and nights lived in those hands of his. She'd watched them as he lifted the spoon and tried to feed her with those hands, gentle enough to care but powerful enough to defend her. She'd felt the tenderness in them as he wiped away her tears with his fingertips.

She closed her eyes as she pressed his palm to her cheek. "You could have done anything else to show your claim to those men. You could have hurt me with your hands like they wanted to. You didn't, though."

"Don't defend me. I don't deserve it," he said

quietly.

Looking up, she shook her head in amazement. What did she have to say to convince him to forgive himself? Then the reality of what needed to be said between them came over her.

"Say it, Nick. Say it and then never say or think it again."

"Say what?"

The time had come for that one horrible event to be put into the past. She would never have anything real with him if he couldn't forgive himself.

"Say what you did to me. Say it so you and I both can see that whatever it needs to be called, you saved me and protected me by doing that. So say it and then let it go forever."

His eyes filled with pain, and his eyebrows drew in toward the center of his face in a look of agony. "No. I won't say it out loud. It's bad enough that word will live in my mind forever. I won't say it and demean you again."

Clutching his hand, she pressed it over her heart. "You have to or you'll never be able to be with me. Is that you want?"

He pulled his hand away and turned his back on her before walking back into the apartment. She followed him, not willing to give up on the future she believed they could have if only he admitted the truth.

"Nick, just say it. Say it and then never let it come between us again," she pleaded, but he refused to face her now.

"Saying a word isn't going to change what happened, Persephone."

"Then say it."

Suddenly, he spun around and she saw pure anguish in his expression. All the kindness had left his eyes, leaving only pain and hurt. "I can't! I can't even admit it to myself without feeling like I hate myself for what I did," he yelled.

But she knew he had to face what actually happened if they were ever to be together, so she would say it.

"Then I will. You raped me. You did it to protect me, but the word is rape. And I forgive you because you didn't think you had a choice. I don't care what the rest of the world would think about that because I know why you did it. But if you can't admit what it was, and it was rape, we have no chance of anything from this point on."

As she spoke, he grimaced and every time she said that word, he reacted like someone had punched him in the face. Finally, when she finished, he started backing away from her.

"Stop...don't do this."

But she followed him, unable to stop because she believed with all her heart that if they didn't get past this, they would have no future. She needed him to admit the truth to her there as she stood in front of him not in judgment but in acceptance.

"Nick, you can't let this tear you up anymore. I forgive you, but if you can't forgive yourself, then how can we ever be together? Don't you care about me? Don't you want to be with me?"

He stopped and shook his head. "You have no idea. I fell in love with you, Persephone. It made no sense, but I fell in love with you during those awful days. I would have done anything to protect you. I would have died for you! And what did I do instead?"

She listened and heard what she'd wanted to hear since they escaped that horrible place. That he loved her like she loved him. Now that he'd admitted that, he hesitated to take the final step that he had to in order for them to be together.

Pain covered his face, and he finally said in a strangled voice that told her just how tortured he'd been over what he did, "I held you down on that bed and raped you while those fucks cheered me on."

Persephone wrapped her arms around him as she pressed her cheek to the spot over his heart. "And you protected me by doing that. Never forget that, Nick. You protected me from them. And then you got me out of that place. You saved me."

He stood stiffly, refusing to embrace her in return as she spoke, but when she finished, he hugged her to him and pressed a kiss to the top of her head. "I'm so sorry, Persephone. I'm so sorry."

She reveled in the feel of his arms around her, protecting her as he had from the minute he met her. What they were wasn't normal or ordinary or what most women would want, but it's what she wanted.

Tilting her head back, she looked up into his dark brown eyes and said what they both needed to hear. "I forgive you. I promise I will never hold that against you. I just need to know that you can forgive yourself."

Nick nodded, and for the first time, he kissed her. Softly and tenderly, his lips pressed against hers, sending waves of sweetness rolling through her. She'd never been kissed so reverently before, like he wanted to worship her with his mouth.

His hands cradled her face, gently keeping her just where she needed to be so they didn't break this first kiss she would remember for the rest of her life. Just as she wondered if all he wanted was an innocent kiss, he pulled her into his body and slid his tongue into her mouth, sending a rush of need to the very center of her being.

Now waves of desire replaced the sweetness from just a minute before as his tongue teased hers with a promise of what he could do with it on other parts of her body. She wanted to feel him on every inch of her, teasing her need into a fever pitch only he could satisfy.

Gently, he stuffed his hand into her hair and tugged her head back so his lips left hers. Desperate for the feel of his mouth kissing her, she made a noise that let him know how much she missed him already.

"Don't stop," she said, not ashamed in the least to beg for another taste of him.

"If you stay now, I'm going to want you in my bed tonight and every night after that, Persephone."

Breathlessly, she whispered the only word that came to her mind when she thought of being his. "Yes."

"There's no turning back," he said in a whisper against her lips.

Once again, she spoke the only word she could. "Yes."

With that, the final barrier he'd kept between them faded into nothingness, and he kissed her long and deep like her lips held the only salvation this world offered someone like him. His hands closed into fists in her hair, tugging harder than before so tiny licks of pain danced across her scalp.

She didn't cry out, wanting to feel every sensation he created in her, and moaned with each time he pulled her hair, silently praying to God he wouldn't suddenly worry about hurting her because of what happened between them at that house weeks before.

He said her name roughly against her lips before lifting her into his arms and walking toward the bedroom, never tearing his gaze from hers as they moved. She searched his eyes for safety while at the same time craving every inch of his body to be on hers.

Nick was her protector, her savior, and now the one man she'd give everything to have inside her.

Gently, he placed her on the bed and stood perfectly still for a moment at the foot of the bed staring down at her. Persephone worried the past haunted him as he said nothing but didn't move toward her.

Extending her hand, she reached out to show him this time wasn't like the last. His gaze slid down her arm to where her fingers stretched to touch him, and then he took her hand and slowly lowered his body down onto hers.

He took care not to let all his weight fall on her and gently kissed her as his hand slid down over her hip. She sensed his worry that he needed to atone for their first sexual experience, but that's not what she wanted.

She wanted the man she knew he was to take

her for his own.

Placing her palms on either side of his face, she looked into his eyes and saw that worry in them. "You don't have to treat me like I'll break if we do this. I'm not going to break, Nick."

His expression hardened for a moment, and then he kissed her long and deep again like before. It made her head swim from desire and need, and she arched her back to feel the hardness of him against her.

Their hands tugged and pulled at the clothes that separated them until they lay skin to skin, bare to one another. Persephone ran her hand down over his chest to his ribs and abs, letting her palm linger on the muscles that led down to a sensual V near his hips. Hard and firm, they made her want to feel more of him.

Nick pushed her legs open with his knee and settled in between them. Looking down at her through half-lidded eyes hazy with need, he pushed his hips forward and filled her slowly until all of him nested inside her. She'd felt him before like this, but now he filled her completely, making her gasp.

She lifted her legs and wrapped them around his waist. Pressing her heels to the small of his back, she urged him to keep going. He took the hint and moved his hips back and forth, easing in and out of her so slowly it nearly made her lose her mind.

His right hand cupped her breast, and he pinched her excited nipple between his thumb and forefinger, sending a jolt of electricity straight to her core. He began thrusting faster and harder, inching her toward a climax she not only wanted but needed from him.

He kissed her, his tongue snaking over her lips to tease her tongue, and with each thrust into her body, he brought her closer to satisfying her in a way she'd never felt before. Faster and faster he pumped into her, making her body race toward that one moment when she completely surrendered to him.

"Persephone," he groaned as his mouth slid from hers down over her jaw to her neck.

The touch of his lips sent a rush through her, but she needed something else. Something more. Finding his hand, she guided it to her neck and closed her eyes as his fingers instinctively closed around her tender skin.

She didn't know if he realized this simple act of his hand on her neck was the only remnant of their previous time together she yearned for. She just understood somewhere deep inside that his hand there had been the only thing that had made it all bearable, allowing her to drown out the noise around them and feel his strong hand powerfully holding her and refusing to let go.

Tilting her head back, she reveled in his control and felt her desire and need overwhelm her. She came hard, her hand holding him there around her neck as her release tore through every inch of her body.

Seconds later, he stilled inside her, and she felt the rush of warmth fill her. Looking down at her, he lay there silently staring at her neck where his hand remained covered by hers.

"I didn't hurt you, did I?" he asked in a low voice that sounded like he dreaded the answer to his question.

Persephone smiled and tilted her head to kiss him softly on the lips. "No. I wouldn't call that hurting me."

He gave her a smile and pushed her hair off her face in a gesture of sweetness she loved. For all that they'd been through, none of it could hurt her as much as not having him right there next to her now.

Chapter Thirteen

Nick slid his hand down between her breasts as Persephone's hand fell away from its hold on him. He stared at the pale skin and saw marks where his fingers had squeezed her tender neck again. He'd wanted this first real time they were together to be sweet, but his body had taken over and before he knew it, he was on top of her thrusting like a savage animal.

Like he had before.

"Please talk to me," she said softly, clearly picking up on how he felt about what he'd just done.

"I didn't mean for it to be like that," he said, avoiding meeting her gaze.

"I couldn't imagine it being any better," Persephone said with a tiny chuckle that made him look up at her.

Her smile seemed genuine, even though their sex had been rougher than he ever wanted it to be. He didn't know how to feel about that. For him, being with a woman always ran along the edge of rough, but he didn't intend for it to be like that with her.

Especially after what happened before.

"Nick, listen to me. I'm not going to break. I told you that, and I meant it. Being with you like that was exactly what I hoped it would be."

"But I didn't mean to be so rough with you," he said, trying to explain but not finding the right words.

She simply smiled and touched his cheek. "You weren't rough. You were exactly what I wanted. And from the point on, you should know I love the feel of your hand around my neck like that."

He couldn't hide his surprise at what she said. He'd intentionally tried to stay away from anything he'd done before, and now she lay there smiling and telling him she loved such a simple but violent action from that horrible time.

"I thought that would…I thought it would remind you of…"

His words trailed off into nothingness when she kissed him, cutting off his train of thought. Pulling away, she smiled up at him.

"The feel of your hand on me and not just you thrusting into me made that bearable then. It's not that I like being choked or anything like that. It's just that feeling your hand touching me helped me push away everything else. I can't explain it any better than that, but I knew the moment you kissed me tonight that all I wanted to feel was your hand touching me there."

Persephone snuggled up against his side and lay her head on his shoulder. Never before with any woman had he felt so at home. No one had ever made him want more until her.

Now that she was in his bed, he never wanted to let her go. He didn't know what that meant to either of them, but whatever he had to do to keep her with him, he'd do it.

He'd gone long enough in this life without feeling what she offered. He didn't want to go another minute without her or how she made him feel like he'd finally come home.

Pressing a kiss to the top of her head, he remembered she'd said she wanted his help with something. "You mentioned you wanted my help with some plan. What is it?"

Whatever it was, he wanted to be a part of it because he'd be with her.

She looked up at him and propped her head up on her hand. "I want to start up a group to help women. I want to find men like you and get them to help women who need it like I did. And I want you by my side when I do this."

Nick loved that out of the horrible experience she'd had, what she wanted to do was help others in similar experiences. He'd never met anyone like

Persephone before, and her kindness made him want to be a part of this new project.

With a smile, he joked, "I'm not sure there are many men like me, but we can give it a shot."

Rolling her eyes, she said, "I didn't mean just like you. You're one of a kind, for sure. But men who are skilled in things you are. I want to set up an organization that can help women wherever they need it. I have more money than I could ever spend, so cost isn't an issue. I'm planning on buying an estate I found out about yesterday. I want that to be the organization's headquarters."

She stopped for a moment and then said, "And I want you to be by my side there. You'd be in charge of the men who work for us, and I'll be the money and contacts part. I might as well use my father's connections for good. Maybe I'll be able to prove people wrong and show them money doesn't have to corrupt."

In all that, the word us stuck out to Nick. Us. The two of them working together to make this plan of hers to help women like he'd helped her come true.

He'd never thought of himself as a particularly honorable man, at least not since what happened that made him leave the bureau. The thought occurred to him that maybe he wasn't the best man for this job.

"I don't know if I'm good enough for this,

Persephone. I'm a hired gun. I have been for years. It sounds like you need someone more for what you have in mind."

Cradling his face, she looked up into his eyes. "You're exactly the man I need for this, Nick. I don't need a saint in my life or in my bed. I need you."

He definitely wasn't a saint.

"Then I guess you came to the right man."

She smiled and kissed him on the cheek. "Do you want to hear what I want to do?"

Enjoying the sight of her so eager and happy about this project, he leaned back on the pillows and folded his arms behind his head. "I can't wait," he said with a smile. "But maybe after another round?"

"I really want to tell you about this, Nick. Sex isn't anything as important as what we're going to do," she said before she kissed him on the lips.

"I'm getting the feeling we need to have a meeting of the minds on this sex thing," he joked.

"You'll have a chance to have me in bed every night for the rest of our lives, but this means a lot to me. I want it to mean a lot to you too."

He knew it was probably the craziest thing he'd ever thought, but something in his gut told him to trust Persephone's vision for this group she wanted to assemble. It had been a long time since he worked with a team. Maybe it was time to stop being a loner once and for all.

Pulling her on top of him, he kissed her long and deep like he'd wanted to every minute since falling for her. She brought out a passion in him for more than he'd had in his life for years, so it felt right to go along with her on this idea of hers.

"Okay. Tell me what you want to do. I'm in."

Her dark eyes opened wide, and she smiled so sweetly he couldn't have stopped himself from loving her if he wanted to. "I can't tell you how much that means to me. It's because of you that I can do this at all. You're the inspiration behind this, Nick. I hope you know that."

Never one to inspire anything, he didn't know what to say to that. "I just did my job, Persephone. I'm not sure I'm any kind of inspiration."

The smile slid from her face, and her expression turned serious as she shook her head. "You were so much more than that. You were sent to rescue me, but you didn't just do that. You gave me hope when I didn't have any. You made those nights and days bearable, Nick. Don't diminish how important you were to me."

Nick didn't know how to react. No one had ever said anything like that to him in his life. Not when he tried to do good whenever he could and stay on the straight and narrow so the bureau would take him. Not when he proudly worked for the FBI trying to protect his country. Certainly not when Tanya was killed and he left it all behind to become a hired gun to anybody with enough money to hire him.

"I just did what I had to do to protect you," he said, not knowing how to tell her how much her words meant to him.

"Well, I want that for any woman who needs help. For the woman who is being stalked by some crazy neighbor or an ex-boyfriend who can't let go, and for the woman who turns to the police but they can't help her because there's not enough proof she's in danger. I want those women to have their Nick like I had mine. I want them to have the hope you gave me. I have the money and the ability to do my part, but this only works if you're by my side helping me. I can't do this without you, and even more, I don't want to. So if you need more convincing, I'm here to tell you I plan on convincing you to do this with me."

He looked at her beautiful brown eyes so full of that hope she claimed he gave her and couldn't say no, even if he wanted to. But he didn't want to. Nick wanted to share that hope she had and let it into his life again.

To believe that he could make a difference once more when it counted most to the one person who made him want to hope again.

"You don't have to convince me. I'm in. All

in."

"All in? I haven't mentioned the fact that you're going to have to convince these guys to live on an estate in rural Virginia."

Nick had a feeling the men he had in mind wouldn't have any problem walking away from their lives and starting over on some multi-million dollar estate. "Don't worry. I'll figure out a way to make them see they should. Paying them handsomely would be a good start."

Persephone smiled broadly. "That I can do. It's one of the benefits of being a very wealthy woman. Anything else you want me to do, just say the word and it's done."

"It must be nice having that much money that you can say something like that and mean it," he joked as he brought her mouth to his in a kiss again.

She tilted her head to the side and chuckled. "The wealthy of this world have a choice to make every day. They can do good with what they've been blessed with or they can act selfishly. I choose to do good, and I choose to do it with you."

He kissed this woman who wanted him to join her in a project that might have been more idealistic than any he'd ever heard of and reveled in the feel of her enthusiasm for doing good as they began to make love again. He had no idea if he could ever live up to who she believed him to be.

But he damn well planned to try every day.

✦ ✦ ✦

PERSEPHONE HELD HIS hand as she led him through the main building on the Blackmore estate she'd dropped over four million on a few weeks before. In that time, he'd been busy setting up the group with men to fill out the ranks of their group, but she'd spent it getting the house ready for everyone. As he looked around in awe at the mere size of the home around him, she eagerly explained how she planned to add on to some areas of the estate and raze a few outside buildings on the edge of the grounds.

"So at first it might feel a little tight with all the men here and us, along with the assistant I plan to bring in, but the workmen will be starting the new building next month, so it won't be too bad," she said in a bubbly voice as Nick tried to take in everything around him.

"Tight?" he asked, stopping in the doorway between what she'd called the great room and another equally as great room in front of him. "How big is this main house?"

"A little over eight thousand square feet," she said casually, as if eight thousand square feet for ten people would be like them all being crammed into a house the size of a shack.

"Holy hell, Persephone. How many bedrooms does this house alone have?"

"Seven, which means at first some of the men are going to have to share quarters. But once the addition is complete, you and I will be able to move into that, so another few thousand feet will be freed up for some more bedrooms for the men."

None of this discussion about thousands of square feet seemed to impress her. She talked about a few thousand square feet like it meant nothing. Nick assumed it had to be because she'd always lived like this, but he knew the type of men he'd bring in and thousands of square feet would likely be the biggest space they'd ever lived in.

"I wouldn't worry about them sharing quarters. Some of them have spent years doing just that."

"Good. Then they won't mind doing it here. They'll have a game room and a place to relax too, along with enough bathrooms for them all, so I think we'll be able to get started sometime in the next few weeks."

She moved to walk into the next room on their grand tour, but Nick pulled her back into his arms. Looking down into her face, he saw just getting this first stage of her plan going thrilled her, and he loved that.

"Hey, let's take a break for a second."

"Don't you want to see the rest of the place?"

"I will. I'd rather just be here with you for a moment," he said before leaning down to kiss her on the lips.

"Do you like the place, Nick?" she asked wide-eyed, like his opinion meant the world to her.

He looked around at the room he stood in and wondered how anyone couldn't like it. It reminded him of some of those European palaces he'd seen on TV some nights when he couldn't get to sleep. Sky-high cathedral ceilings made the living spaces feel even bigger than the actual square footage. The walnut hardwood floors, newly refinished, grounded the rooms and gave them warmth. She'd told him all she'd been up to, but until he saw it for himself, he hadn't believed the estate would be this impressive. It had more bedrooms and bathrooms than all the places he lived in over the past decade combined. For someone like him, this estate or anywhere like it could never be even a dream because it just sat too far out of reach.

"I like it if you like it," he said, keeping the real truth of how impressed it all made him hidden.

Reaching up, she caressed his cheek and kissed him. "I want this to work, and I'm willing to spend my last dime to see it happen. The men you're bringing in deserve a nice place to live. People who put their lives on the line to help others shouldn't have to live in a rundown house. I just want them to be appreciated for the good they do."

"Have you always been this way?" Nick wondered aloud, curious how a woman who had been given everything in life could be so generous with herself.

Persephone thought about the question for a moment and answered, "I don't know. All I know is that on the first night back at my parents' house, all I wanted was two things. I wanted to be with you, and I wanted to help other women like you helped me. Now that we're here and you're finding men to work with us, I've made both of those dreams come true."

Taking her face in his hands, he kissed her and wondered how he'd been so lucky to have the love of someone like her. He didn't know what he'd done in his life to deserve her.

"I must have been a saint in a past life or something because you're way too good for me," he said with a smile, knowing how true that statement was.

But she shook her head like she always did when he said things like that. "Come on. Let's take a look at the game room these guys will get. I ordered a new pool table that was delivered yesterday, and the designer persuaded me to get a foosball table, although I have no idea what that is. Do you know?"

Nick chuckled at how her background sometimes made ordinary everyday things sound so foreign when she talked about them. "Yeah. I'm sure the guys will love it. I might even have to spend some time in this game room."

"Should I have told her to get two foosball tables?" she asked as she tugged him into another pretty damn great room.

With a smile, he brought her hand to his lips and kissed it. "No. I'll be fine."

"Okay. Well, just wait until you see the kitchen. With all those people living here, I made sure to get an industrial refrigerator and two stoves. I still need to find a cook, but don't worry. I'm on it. But the kitchen is absolutely perfect."

As he followed her through one room into the next and she talked about how much she loved the blue and soft white color scheme she chose for the kitchen, a sense of pride in what she wanted to accomplish with this place welled in his chest. Sure, maybe she enjoyed redecorating a house the size of a small state, but he believed in his heart she wanted to do this for the good it would help them do in the world.

And he had the right men for the job. He had

a few lined up already, so it wouldn't be long before he brought them all here so they could start fulfilling Persephone's dream of helping women in danger.

He knew from far too much experience that there would be no shortage of them, unfortunately. Seven men might not be able to save everyone, but it was a damn good start and he was proud to be a part of it.

Chapter Fourteen

Persephone checked her makeup and hair in the mirror one last time before heading down to the great room to meet the seven men Nick had settled on in just the past week. He didn't tell her much about them other than the files he offered to show they had the skills necessary to do the job they needed them for, so all she knew was on paper each of them looked like perfect choices.

She trusted him with this job like she'd trusted him with her life. If he believed in these seven men, then she did. Meeting them now was more of a formality.

If Nick wanted these men on the team, then they were part of the team already.

The bedroom door opened and he peeked his head in. "Ready? You've got an audience waiting for you."

Turning away from her reflection, she looked over at him and smiled. "I'm ready. I can't wait to meet them, Nick. I've already got two leads on women who need our help right now, and I expect to hear about more leads later this afternoon. Your team is already very much in demand."

He held the door open for her, and as she walked past him, he snaked his arm around her waist and pulled her to his body. "Have I ever mentioned how much I love your passion for this project?"

Few things made her happier than having his support for her idea. She knew far too many men would have dismissed it as a female problem or a flight of fancy she'd get over. But Nick wasn't one of those men, and his help and encouragement from the first he heard of her plan helped her make it come to fruition.

"Have I mentioned how this would have never come about without you by my side?" she asked in response to his question.

He simply smiled and kissed her sweetly. "Time to go meet them."

Remembering the files on each man, she hurried back into the bedroom to grab the stack of dossiers she'd left on the nightstand. "I want to have them so I can put names to faces and information."

With a smile, Nick said, "I don't think you'll have to worry about that. I have a feeling you'll be able to keep them straight after today. They're a pretty unique group."

As they walked down the hallway to the main house, she wondered what that comment meant. She trusted Nick implicitly, but she didn't know how she felt about the adjective he'd used to describe them. Unique. It rarely meant anything positive when it was used to describe anything other than artwork, and even then it was often negative.

"Unique? Should I be worried?"

Nick shook his head. "Nope. You don't have to worry about anything. I'll handle whatever needs to be handled."

Unique made her wonder, but mentioning something might need to be handled made Persephone downright nervous. The women they intended on helping didn't have time for things to be handled with these unique men.

She stopped him in front of the door to the great room and took his hand in hers. Looking up at him, she hoped he understood how much this project meant to her. "I trust you with my life, Nick, but the way you're talking about these men is making me nervous. Promise me they're right for this."

Nodding, he brought her hand to his mouth and kissed her knuckles in that way that never failed to make her feel adored. "I know how much this means to you, Persephone. This has become as important to me as it is to you. I would never let anyone ruin this for you. These men will do you proud. Trust me."

There, in those two words, she heard what she needed to believe in the men he'd chosen.

"I love you and I trust no one in the world more than you, Nick. You saved my life. I hope you don't think I ever doubted you. I just got a little skittish when you said they were unique and you'd handle any issues with them. It never meant that I didn't trust you with everything I believe in."

He kissed her hand again and nodded. "Okay. Ready to meet the team?"

She smiled and took a deep breath. "I'm ready."

Nick opened the large wooden door and escorted Persephone into the great room where the seven men awaited them. Some stood near the fireplace and the windows, while the others sat on the oversized couch and chairs positioned around the coffee table.

Immediately, she noticed how large all of them were. Nick towered over her by nearly a foot at six foot four, but a few of these men looked even bigger than him. The one who stood next to the enormous grey stone fireplace at the far end of the room looked like he himself could physically move the thing with little effort.

"Gentleman, let me introduce you to Persephone Gilmore, the woman behind the organization you just joined," Nick announced in a deep voice full of pride she heard loud and clear.

The men nodded as each one was introduced to her by name and his former job before becoming one of their team. First up, he pointed at the tall man with nearly black hair and dark eyes who stood on the left side of the window across from them dressed in jeans and a dark t-shirt that showed off his very muscular arms. His serious expression bordered on angry as he listed to his introduction.

"Roman Gregory, Army Ranger. You want a man who can handle any situation, among other things, he's your man."

Persephone smiled at him and looked at the folder containing information Nick had collected on him. Scanning the information, she saw he was unattached but had a girlfriend who was killed while he was serving. No girlfriend since. Expert shot.

Lifting her gaze, she nodded her approval. "It's nice to meet you, Roman."

The man said nothing but simply bowed his head in response. The one word that flashed through Persephone's mind for him was impressive.

Pointing toward the man who sat on the end

of the couch furthest away from where they stood, Nick said, "Next up is Hunter McKay. Worked as an LA detective for five years."

She sized up this second man as he stood to approach her. Tall with light brown hair and green eyes, he had an athletic look to him for a man she knew from his dossier was thirty-two years old. Before she could reread the other details on him, he offered her his hand.

"Great to meet you, Persephone. Glad to be on board."

Looking down at his hand wrapped around hers, she appreciated his confidence. A woman in danger needed a man who could control a problem, and she had a feeling Hunter had confidence in spades.

"Good to have you with us, Hunter."

He returned to the couch to sit near the next man to be introduced. Nick pointed toward a muscular man with black hair and stunning deep blue eyes. She had to admit he had a feel to him. It wasn't confidence so much as flair.

She didn't know how she felt about that, though.

"I'd like you to meet Gideon Roberts, Navy SEAL and expert in hand-to-hand combat."

Gideon stood to shake her hand and flashed her a gorgeous smile. "Good to meet you. As soon as Nick told me about all of this, I wanted in."

Obviously brave and downright stunning in jeans and a teal blue button down dress shirt, he reminded Persephone of one of the models she'd seen on a calendar in the nurses' lounge at the hospital. Something about him made her wonder if the man she trusted with her own life knew anything else that he brought to the team. She didn't need a playboy messing with some woman's heart as he helped her escape some terrible danger.

"Thanks, Gideon. Nice to have you here."

Next, Nick pointed at the man who sat next to Gideon. Not as muscular as the others, he had a more intellectual feel to him. His dirty blond hair and pale blue eyes gave him a more casual look than the others too, even though he wore dress pants and a white button-down shirt that cried out for a tie.

"Persephone, let me introduce you to Xavier Martin, our resident IT pro," Nick said as the man stood to shake her hand.

"It's very nice to meet you, Miss Gilmore. Nick might be building me up a little much, though. IT professional sounds like something my mother would make me put on my resume. My real title would be hacker, if we're being honest here."

Xavier had a lilt to his voice that made him sound so much friendlier than any of the other men. Persephone had never met a real life hacker before and couldn't help but admit to herself that she would have thought one would look far scarier in person.

"Nice to have you here with us, Xavier."

Still focused on the only hacker she'd ever met, she didn't hear Nick introduce the next member of the team. Following where his finger aimed toward the window, she saw a man standing near Roman with closely cropped dark hair and olive skin dressed in a dark grey suit. He had a look to him that struck Persephone as exotic.

Turning to look at Nick, she whispered, "Who is this?"

"Julian. Julian Cain. Jack of all trades and master of several of them."

"Like?" she asked, wondering why Nick seemed reluctant to tell her more about this man. She looked down at the file she had on him and found little more than just his vital statistics and that he'd worked with Nick on a number of cases in the past when he was with the FBI.

"Let's just say Julian here has a way of knowing how to handle people," Nick answered cryptically. "Julian, this is Persephone Gilmore."

She swiveled her head to see him walking toward her with a smile on his face. "It's very nice to meet you, Julian."

The rest of the men stared at him like she did, likely thinking the same thing that was running through her mind. What was this man's skill?

He took hold of her hand and held it instead of shaking it like all the other men had. After a moment, it felt awkward, but when she looked at him to let him know he could let go, he locked his gaze on hers.

"I get the feeling you're not sure about me. That's okay. I don't mind proving myself. Also, Nick didn't seem to want to tell you the whole truth about me. I would be what you would call a con man. Well, a potential con man. I keep on the right side of the law for the most part. Counting cards is one of my talents. I also have a photographic memory. Your man and I used to work together on cases when he was in the bureau, so he can vouch for my skills."

His voice had a hypnotic sound to it, and Persephone found herself feeling like she had been put under a spell by the time he finished speaking. Or maybe it was how his deep brown eyes stared at her so intently, like he was searching her face for some answer to a question.

Nick pulled her hand away from Julian's and slid his arm around her waist. "And that's Julian. Save the act for when we serve drinks."

The man chuckled wickedly and stepped back, putting his hands up in front of him as he did. "No problem, boss. I didn't mean to step on any toes."

Ignoring his apology, Nick moved on to the man sitting in the chair. "And this is Marius Grisham, former CIA black ops. He's the epitome of the underground man. Expert at infiltration. If you want to find someone, he's your man."

Persephone focused her attention on the man who seemed to suddenly appear in front of her. Dressed in black dress pants and a white button down shirt, he looked like he could handle himself as well as any of the other men. Quiet confidence practically oozed out of every pore and his impressive size added to that feeling.

"It's nice to meet you, Marius," she said as she extended her hand to shake his much larger hand.

"Very nice to be here, Persephone. I have to say I was intrigued when Nick told me what you had in mind, and if this place is any indication of how this all will be run, I can see myself fitting in just fine."

She smiled, happy that all her efforts to make their home base everything she thought they'd need hadn't gone unnoticed by at least one of them. "I want you all to have a place that lets each one of you do this job as effectively as possible. Everything I spend my money on is in pursuit of one goal. To help the women who need you."

Marius smiled and looked around the great

room. "I like the way you think."

Of all of the men, Persephone had a feeling she might end up liking Marius the most. He seemed to appreciate her efforts, and she liked that.

"Finally, the one holding up the fireplace over there is Dax Sturgis, one of my closest friends from the bureau and a whiz at forensics, among many other things."

Nick smiled at his old friend, and Persephone watched as the enormous man slowly walked toward her. As confident and assured as the others, he smiled warmly at her as he shook her hand. She couldn't help but notice how good looking he was with his dark hair and his chiseled cheekbones and strong jaw, even though he wore red workout pants and a yellow t-shirt with some bar's logo on it that resembled something vaguely sexual.

"It's good to meet the woman who got this guy to give up that life of rootlessness. We former bureau guys need something honorable to keep us out of trouble. I'm happy you're giving him and me a chance to do good again."

Persephone wanted to look down at the folders in her left hand to find out more about Dax so she could know what he'd been up to since leaving the bureau if he hadn't been spending his time like Nick. She made a mental note to read up on him after this meeting.

Dax made his way back to his position next to the fireplace, and she began to address the group on what she wanted this project to achieve. She knew she had lofty goals for the team, but she believed they could do it.

She had to. The women they would help couldn't afford for them to fail.

"I know Nick has told you what this team will do, but let me give you my speech on it. This is not just something this rich girl has decided to do with her money for the time being until something more interesting or sexier comes along. I know what women go through, and if it hadn't been for Nick, I might still be held hostage in that house my kidnappers had me at. Or worse, I'd be dead."

She looked at the man she loved and smiled. "But he was there to help me when I needed him. There are women across this country who need help like that every day. Some go to the police and are told there isn't anything they can do until the person stalking them or the person threatening them actually harms them. That's unacceptable. The policy of being reactive puts women in more harm. I want this team to be as proactive as possible. The minute I hear a woman is in danger, one of you will be assigned the job of protecting her and helping her get away from whoever and whatever is threatening her."

Xavier raised a finger and asked, "How do you hear about these women needing help? No offense, but from what I know of you, there's no connection to law enforcement in your past."

She did enjoy when people underestimated her. Nodding, she acknowledged the truth of what he'd said.

"You're right. I haven't been involved in law enforcement whatsoever, but I am the daughter of one of the most powerful news media giants in the world. My father's connections with police forces around the country will pave the way. Already through my dealings with some of them, I've found them more than eager to pass along information about women in danger they wish they could do more for. There's not a cop in this nation who wants to see a woman hurt, but often the laws tie their hands. Since this organization will be outside law enforcement, those laws imposed on the police won't affect you."

She heard one of the men murmur "extra-legal" under his breath and quickly moved to quash any ideas that she had assembled a group of vigilantes.

"I'm not here to say I will condone anyone breaking the law. I won't. But this group won't be forced to concern themselves with the rights of men who want to terrorize women. Your only concern will be protecting the client and ensuring she's safe and out of harm's way."

Roman cleared his throat and asked in a low voice tinged with disgust, "Are we talking about us being bodyguards here then?"

Persephone shook her head. "No. Your work is going to be of far more consequence. A woman being stalked needs more than just a bodyguard. She needs someone to help her find out who's out there who wants to do her harm, if she doesn't already know. On the other hand, a woman being threatened might know who's trying to harm her. Your job is to not only protect her but find out what's behind the threats. If we just wanted bodyguards, we could have hired bouncers. I'm paying you all top dollar for far more and expect you to use your considerable skills each one of you brings to the table on every assignment."

She sensed as Roman nodded and leaned back against the windowsill that she'd given him an answer he could respect. Scanning the room, she saw the men's expressions said they liked what they were hearing.

"I'm sure there will be many questions, but for now, I want to thank you for joining Nick and me in this. We're dedicated to seeing this succeed. You'll find your rooms have been stocked with everything you could possibly need, in addition to the kitchen having enough food in every variety to feed an army. The cook's name is Summers, and he works from six in the morning to six at night. After that, you're on your own to cook whatever food you like. Everything will be taken care of for you—housekeeping, laundry, and meals. Your salaries will be deposited into the accounts you provided. Other than that, there is a game room equipped with whatever you may want to play in your off time and a media room where films can be shown. I have some connections in that area, so first run movies are available."

She stopped as they all seemed to hang on every word she spoke. She knew how good they'd have it there, but if she wanted to get the best out of them for their clients, she had to offer them more than just money.

Because what they gave up to be a part of Project Artemis was a hefty price.

"One final note. You may come and go from this place as you like. There are cars enough for everyone. Each of you knows how to lay low and stay out of the limelight. That's one of the reasons you were chosen. But in exchange for all you have here, there is one requirement. You must remain unattached. If at any point you decide that your love life is more important than your job, you will have to resign your position. Other than living here, which won't be too much of a hardship for anyone, your remaining single is the only other non-negotiable. If that's impossible for anyone, please let us know now and you can leave. No harm, no foul. If not, the first assignments will be handed out today."

She waited for any of them to speak up and say they couldn't abide by the rules, but not a single one did. Nick had told her he made sure to only recruit men he knew could accept the structure of the job, but she'd wanted to make sure. Giving up the chance of being in a relationship would certainly give her pause. She knew it was a lot to ask of the team, but she needed their focus to be entirely on the women they would help.

"Please feel free to take a look around after you find your rooms. Lunch will be served at noon precisely. Summers told me he was preparing a huge country ham, so be sure to come to the table hungry."

Persephone thanked them and turned to face Nick. "I'm going to the office. I want to discuss things with you before any assignments are given out."

"I'll be there in a minute."

As she left the room, she felt good about this group of men. She only hoped they'd do for their clients what Nick did for her.

Chapter Fifteen

Nick opened the door to the office he and Persephone shared and smiled at the scene in front of him. Hard at work, she tapped away at the keys on her laptop, truly a woman on a mission.

"So what do you think?" he asked her about the team he'd assembled.

Her fingers stilled and she looked up at him with intensity in her eyes. "Well, I'm not all together sure about all of them, but for now, I think we're off to a good start."

He stopped at her mention of not being sure about the men he'd assembled. "Which ones?"

Persephone raised her eyebrows. "A con man? I mean, he clearly can physically handle himself. All of them look like they can. But I got the sense he's more carnival barker than I think I'm comfortable with."

Chuckling, Nick thought back to how many times he'd heard Julian described in similar terms. "Well, I can tell you his ability to understand the psyche of criminals and his photographic memory have come in handy more than a few times when we worked together. I think if you give him a chance, you'll see why I brought him on board."

She twisted her face into a grimace. "And Gideon has something about him that I'm not sure of. Maybe it's the way he looks. I'm a little worried he's more playboy than what we need."

Nick mentally made a note to never let Gideon find out that Persephone had called him a playboy. The guy would just be too damn pleased with himself that a woman thought of him that way.

"I can tell you that he's a world class bust ass too, but remember he was a Navy SEAL. That's got to count for whole hell of a lot. Trust me. He'll be fine."

A slow smile spread across her lips. "I trust no one more in the world, Nick, so of course I'll give both of them a chance."

"Good. I think the team we have to start with will be able to handle whatever assignments come up."

"I hope so," she said, pointing at her laptop screen. "We've got three clients who need our help already. One in D.C., one in Miami, and one in a small town about an hour outside of St. Paul, Minnesota."

He walked around her desk and stood behind

her to read the details of the cases already waiting for the men. Leaning down, he placed his hands on Persephone's shoulders and scanned the page in front of him.

The client in D.C. had appealed for help from the police but to no avail. She'd run up against the old boy network that protected politicians, and the man was now threatening not only her career as a congressional staffer but her life.

"How did we find out about this case?"

Smiling, Persephone leaned back against his body and looked up at him. "Not everyone in the D.C. police kowtows to the politicians."

"My faith in the system is momentarily restored," Nick said with a smile as he looked down into her beautiful eyes so full of focus.

"And the other two?" he asked as he skimmed through the details about a woman in Miami being stalked by an ex-boyfriend who just happened to be a professional basketball player and another woman in Minnesota in hiding after accusing her boss of sexual harassment and then being the victim of a suspicious home invasion that seemed more to scare her than to steal anything.

"In the past month, I've reached out to police forces in every major city in the US, and I'm halfway through my list of smaller cities. I also have people at every one of my father's newspapers who have promised to contact me if they know of any woman in trouble. It's a start, at least."

Nick bent over her and kissed her softly on the lips. "It's more than a start, Persephone. I just hope we can keep up with all the requests we're going to get."

"Me too. Rome wasn't built in a day is what I keep telling myself, but I don't want to let anyone down either."

The concern that she'd disappoint someone in need etched itself into her face and drew her mouth down into a frown. He'd seen that same expression on her face every day she sat tied to that chair, and he hated seeing her look like that now just as much as he had then.

It made him want to do whatever it took to get rid of that worry that showed so clearly on her beautiful face.

He kissed her and then crouched down next to her chair. She looked down at him with anticipation in her eyes.

"What? You seem like you want to say something."

Shaking his head, he smiled at this incredible woman who sat before him. Out of the most horrible experience of her life, she'd taken all the good she could find in it and turned it into something great. He'd admired people before, but he could honestly say the pride he felt for what she was building there made his heart swell.

"I just want you to know how proud I am of you. You could have come away from that kidnapping and turned inward, and you know what? No one would have blamed you. But you didn't. You took what they did to you and made something good happen from it. That's damn incredible, if you ask me."

Persephone shook her head. "You always neglect to mention your part in all of this, Nick. You're the inspiration for everything I'm doing. I want to do everything in my power to ensure that any woman in danger has her own Nick there for her. This all came about because you pulled me out of that place. Don't ever forget that."

As always, hearing her say those things touched him, but he preferred to give her all the credit. "I was just doing my job. You're doing something incredible. There's the difference."

She slid her hands over his cheeks and looked into his eyes with love in hers. "This humility thing you have going on isn't necessary with me. I was there with you at that house. I know what happened."

And there was the truth that he couldn't escape. He still hadn't forgiven himself for that one horrible day, but they went through it together. Now, he looked forward to Project

Artemis and all they would accomplish together in the future.

Pressing his forehead to hers, he whispered, "I love you, Persephone. I hope you know that."

His declaration was rewarded with one of her tender smiles that never failed to make his heart skip a beat.

"And I love you. Are you ready to give out these first assignments?"

He sat back on his heels and nodded. "Let's get to helping these women."

For the first time since he left the bureau, he felt like he was involved in something honorable. It may never make up for the mistakes he made in the past, but it made him look forward to the future.

And he hadn't felt that for far too long.

NICK HEARD THE men as the delivery guys brought in the new poker table and chairs to the game room. He'd kept this surprise for last because he knew it would be the best one of all. For far too long, they'd all played their favorite game on that dining room table of his at his apartment. Now they'd have a proper table to play on and comfortable chairs too.

He opened the door and saw them all staring at the new addition to the room. The delivery men finished setting it all up and walked out, leaving them standing there with their mouths hanging open looking at the enormous oblong table made to order just for their poker games.

"Nice, huh?" he said with a smile as he ran his hand across the back of one of the black leather chairs. "I thought about getting the round table, but with all of us, I figured the eight footer would be better."

Gideon and Xavier practically jumped into chairs on each side of the table, staking their claim on their spots as the rest of the team stood ogling at the newest perk that came from working for Project Artemis. Both men ran their hands over the soft leather chair arms and seemed clearly pleased by Nick's idea.

"You sure do know how to live," Gideon said with a smile. "I like the effect your lady has had on you already. This table and these chairs are the shit!"

"Yeah! Let's play," Xavier said as he rummaged through the drawers under the table to find the chips Nick had ordered to go with the new set.

Each man sat down in his usual place they liked back at his apartment, and Julian chose a spot directly across from Nick on the other end of the oblong table since this was his first time playing with all of them. Running his hands along the mahogany wood trim, he shook his head and grinned.

"Do we have Persephone to thank for this or you?" Julian asked.

Xavier turned to look at Nick and pointed at him. "If you tell me she bought this for us after the big screen TV, pool table, and foosball table, I swear to God I might have to go to her office and tell her I love her, dude. This is like the ultimate man cave now."

Nick chuckled and for a moment thought about how Persephone would react if Xavier actually professed his love for her because of the game room. "This one is all me. Her designer suggested everything else, but I figured since we're going to be playing poker here now, we might as well do it in style."

Marius nodded his approval. "You did good, my friend. I'm not as big a fan of all that other stuff these guys love, but this is what a man should have to play poker. Too bad Dax isn't here to enjoy this inaugural game."

Roman began shuffling the cards. "Bad for Dax but good for me. I don't leave until later tonight, so I get to see if I can win some of the money I lost to you guys last time we played."

Xavier spread the stacks of chips out in front of him and held up a purple one. "What's this?"

"You're in the big leagues now, X," Hunter

said with a chuckle. "That's a five hundred dollar chip."

For a moment, the young hacker looked a little surprised. They'd always only played with white chips for a dollar, red for five, blue for ten, green for twenty-five, and black for a hundred.

"Five hundred, huh? Well, when in Rome," Xavier said with a cocky grin as he began to parse out the chips to each player like he usually did in their games.

As Roman began to deal out the first cards of five card stud, he looked over at Julian. "You play much poker?"

Nick watched as a slow smile spread across Julian's face. "Oh, you know. Here and there."

He hadn't played before with him, but Nick had a feeling a man who had a photographic memory and experience counting cards would be able to hold his own just fine with the rest of them around the poker table.

"Well, since this isn't blackjack, I think we're safe," Nick joked as he picked up his hole card to see what he got to match the seven of spades he had in his face up card.

An ace of diamonds. Certainly not the worst way to start a game.

He scanned the table and saw he had the lowest face up card, so he tossed a red chip into the center of the table. He had an ace, but better to start off slow. Their games had a tendency to go all night.

"I'm in for five."

As everyone placed their bets, Marius asked, "So Persephone doesn't have a problem with you spending your night here with us playing poker?"

Before he could answer, Gideon joked, "If it's Nick, it's losing at poker."

Some things never changed.

Roman began dealing out the third card of the hand to everyone, and Nick saw he got a king of diamonds to go with his ace. Maybe Gideon would be proven wrong tonight.

Looking over at Marius, he said, "She had a few deliveries for the bedroom she wanted to deal with, so I'm sure she's not missing me at all."

No sooner had the word bedroom left his mouth, Gideon and Xavier began ribbing him with their sexual innuendo. Those two certainly never changed.

But as the game continued and he saw Roman deal him a king of hearts to go with his king of diamonds, he didn't care as much that the two bust asses were at it again. Tossing out a blue chip into the pile, Nick liked his chances tonight.

Especially since both Gideon and Xavier both had garbage cards facing up on the table.

"Ten? You must have something good," Hunter joked as he matched the bet.

Nick smiled but didn't say a thing. He had more than something good now. He had a team of men he respected that he led doing the kind of work he'd always wanted to do. Even more, he had Persephone, someone he could finally share his life with.

He definitely had more than good in his life now.

EPILOGUE

AFTER A LONG day of the seven new men getting used to being at the estate, Persephone knew more than ever she needed an assistant. Not that she didn't appreciate the men Nick had brought on to Project Artemis, but dealing with all of them had proven to be exhausting, and it was only the first full day.

Climbing into her brand new tub, she closed her eyes as the hot water enveloped her, easing away the stress of the day moment by moment. Persephone slid her back down the smooth porcelain of the soaker tub until the water and lavender scented bubbles covered up to her chin.

She would have to get used to having all these people around her home from now on. For three years, she'd lived alone in her two-bedroom apartment and had gotten accustomed to being by herself.

But now all that had changed, and in exchange for her independence, she had a team of professionals who would help her achieve the goal that had become everything to her. That trade off was more than worth it, even if all that testosterone threatened to take over the estate after just one day.

"What is it with women and baths?" she heard Nick ask with a chuckle.

She opened her eyes to see him leaning against the doorframe a few feet away. Smiling at her, he repeated his question. "I'm serious. What is it with baths with women? Is it the bubbles?"

Lifting her arm out of the bubbly water, she smiled and blew a handful of suds toward him. "It's a way to relax. You men have watching sports and eating chicken wings, and we women have soaker tubs full of bubbles. You don't see me questioning your love of greasy chicken, do you?"

Nick took a step into the room and stopped. "So this is the famous tub you were talking about this morning. That explains why I haven't seen you for hours."

"You haven't seen me for hours because I needed a break from all those men. There's a cloud of testosterone hanging over this house and the whole estate. If I don't get some women around me quick, this place is going to drive me out of my mind. I figured they'd all stay in their part of the house, but everywhere I turned today, one of them was there. In the kitchen when I wanted to grab an iced tea, Gideon and Xavier were there having some kind of heated discussion about which way hot dogs should be cooked. I thought it was going to end up in a fist fight."

Nick began slowly unbuttoning his grey dress shirt. With a sexy smile that never failed to make her want him, he explained, "On a grill is the only right answer, unless you don't have a grill, which we do. Then, and only then, are you allowed to boil them. Never fried."

Rolling her eyes at this obsession with hot dog cooking, she continued. "Later on, I went for a walk outside to get some fresh air and Hunter and Roman were having some discussion about shooting on their way to the range. I didn't hear much of what they were saying, but one of them had some problem with the other doing something with his gun. After a few minutes of listening to them, I just came back in. I swear all these men do is butt heads."

Persephone watched as Nick tossed his shirt onto the vanity near him and began to unbuckle his belt. She suddenly worried she sounded ungrateful for all he'd done to gather up the men who would work for them on Project Artemis.

"Please don't think I don't like them, Nick. It's just going to take some getting used to."

He smiled and pushed off his shoes. "I'm sure it will be fine."

As he stepped out of his black pants and boxer

briefs, she watched in rapt attention, loving the sight of his muscular body. "I don't want you to think I don't like them or what they're going to do for the group."

Shaking his head, he tossed his dark dress socks over next to his shoes. "I don't think that."

Without another word, he climbed into the tub behind her and wrapped his arms around her shoulders as he sat down. She'd noted the size of this particular tub before she ordered it, thinking it would be perfect for two people as well as one. As Nick situated himself now, she had to admit she'd been right.

It was perfect.

His lips touched the tender skin under her ear, sending shivers down her spine. Nick wove his fingers through hers and whispered, "I was completely wrong about this tub thing."

Persephone turned to look at him and saw him smiling. "Oh yeah. Why?"

He shrugged. "I had no idea how great a bath could be. I've always been a shower kind of guy."

"Are we talking about baths or something else?" she asked, noticing the sparkle in his eyes.

She felt his hard cock press against the small of her back, and then he chuckled low and deep. "Something else," he answered with a sexy grin.

Nick gently spun her around to face him and positioned her legs on either side of his body so she sat just where he needed her to. Setting his hands on her hips, he lifted her as he tilted his hips to slide into her achingly slowly.

Persephone watched as his cock disappeared inside her, filling her completely. Looking up at him, she couldn't help think he looked like a perfect specimen of manhood.

"Mmmm…I swear you're trying to torture me," she said, moaning at how good he felt beneath her. Against her. Inside her.

"No torture. Just taking my time. After a long day at work, there's nothing better than fucking the woman you love slowly to make it last."

Rolling her hips, she leaned forward and kissed him. "What if the woman you love wants things to move a little faster?"

At that moment, what she really wanted was to ride him with utter abandon until the two of them came so hard they collapsed. His hands holding her hips in place made that impossible, but that didn't mean she wouldn't be able to in a minute or so. All he needed was a little convincing.

Nick grinned. "So some wild fucking is on the menu tonight? Hmmm…sounds good to me."

Suddenly, he pulled back from her so his cock nearly left her and then thrust his hips forward so he completely filled her once again. He licked his lips and moaned, "Something like that?"

"Oh yeah," she said in his ear. "Exactly like that."

He slid his hands down over her ass and squeezed her cheeks hard as he began pumping into her, the sound of their bodies joining and the water moving around them making her even more excited.

Persephone loved when they were alone and Nick dropped the aloofness he tended to show others. She'd known from the first time he looked into her eyes as she sat tied to that chair that the man behind the façade was so much more.

With each thrust into her body, he claimed her once again just as he did back in that house. Over time, she'd watched him accept what he'd done, and even though she had a feeling he still hadn't forgiven himself, he never showed her that anymore.

Now when they made love, he was simply a man consumed with giving her pleasure and reveling in their time together.

He looked up at her and smiled wickedly in that way that never failed to make her weak with need. "I love watching you ride me. You know that?"

Raising herself up onto her knees, she teased the head of his cock for a long moment before she slowly slid down, taking all of him inside her. He tilted his head back and groaned low, like the sound came from somewhere deep inside him.

"Oh God…that's it. Right there, baby."

Tracing her finger down over his Adam's apple, Persephone delighted in how sensual he looked lying there as she slid up and down his cock. She could watch him like that for the rest of her life.

She rolled her hips and heard him sigh. "Oh God. Jesus, Seph. You're killing me."

"That's a good thing," she said with a satisfied smile.

Nick lifted his head and arched a single dark brow. "I think we should move to somewhere else."

He looked around the bathroom and smiled as he lifted the two of them out of the tub. "Not that I don't love some underwater sex, but let's head for dry land."

She tightened her thighs against his sides while he walked the two of them across the white marble tile floor of their enormous all-white bathroom and into the bedroom. Whatever he had in mind, she just hoped he hurried up because she had been so close just a few seconds before he decided they needed to change locations.

"Oh, God…hurry, Nick…we don't have to go exotic here. The bed's fine," she whimpered, clinging to him as need made her body ache.

He chuckled and lowered her back down onto the bed. Feeling the blue silk comforter against her skin, she watched his gaze roll over her body until their eyes met and once again, he owned her.

Every part of her, body and soul.

Looking into her eyes, "Tell me what you want, Seph. Let me hear you tell me what you need."

Reaching out for him, she took his hand in hers and brought it to her neck. Just the touch of his fingers to her skin made her desperately want him inside her.

"Make me yours."

Those three little words told him everything he needed to know. He slid into her until there was nothing left of him or her. There in the home where they dedicated their lives to helping others, they joined together to form one.

One heart. One soul. One love.

And like every time since they admitted their feelings that night at his apartment all those months ago, she found the protection Nick freely offered something so integral to her life now that she couldn't imagine living without it.

Or him.

As the two of them rushed toward that delicious sensual edge and toppled over it, he looked down into her eyes with possessiveness that came from claiming her once again.

He pushed back the hair off her face and pressed a gentle kiss onto her forehead. "Now that's what I call ending the day right."

Persephone ran her hand over his hand still resting against her neck and looked around. "I just realized that our room isn't that far away from the rest of the house. Someone might have heard us. Those builders need to get moving on our new room."

Nick laughed and collapsed onto the bed next to her. "I wouldn't worry. Between the foosball and pool tables, the big screen TV, and the shooting range, I'm guessing none of the guys were paying attention to anything we're doing here."

She thought about it for a few moments and did have to admit they had more than enough to amuse them at the house. But would those things make up for what they gave up?

Rolling over to face Nick, she asked, "Do you think they're going to miss not being able to be in relationships?"

He smiled broadly and turned his head to look at her. "They're not going to be monks, Seph. They'll be with women. You just made it a rule they couldn't settle down. I think their lives will continue pretty much the way they've always been. It's not like any of them have been tied down before."

The thought of all that testosterone needing to have an outlet somewhere ran through her mind. She shook her head to get rid of it quickly. "Well, I don't care what they do as long as they're here when we need them for an assignment. I do have to admit I hadn't considered that part of hiring all those men."

Nick slid his tongue over his lower lip and grinned. "Sex, you mean?"

"Well, yeah," she admitted, now suddenly unable to think of anything else about the seven men who lived on the other side of the house.

"I don't think you have to worry. The only man you have to be concerned about here is me, and I'm perfectly happy right where I am."

Persephone smiled and had to admit how content she was to be there with him. They had been through a nightmare no one else could understand, and they'd come out the other side together.

Now when Persephone closed her eyes at night, the darkness didn't terrify her because she knew Nick lay there at her side ready to protect her no matter what. He'd been willing to lay down his life to save hers once before. That he'd do it again she had no doubt.

Pressing his forehead to hers, he whispered the words that never failed to make her happier than she'd ever been in her life.

"I love you, Persephone."

She cradled his face in her hands and looked into his eyes to see the truth they held. "I love you. I owe everything I have to you, Nick. Never forget that."

What he meant to her went beyond just love. He'd saved her life, and for the rest of hers to honor him, she planned to make it possible that other women would feel the safety and protection she felt every moment since he took her out of that house and gave her back her freedom.

He didn't believe he'd done anything more than what he should, but that showed how good a man he was. As she'd told him, she didn't need a saint in her life or in her bed.

She needed him.

Artemis. After spending years as an Army Ranger, he's committed to helping women in danger. He's one of the members Nick and Persephone can always rely on to solve a case and get the client's life back to normalcy because he never lets anyone get in his way of handling a problem. And he never lets anyone get close.

Then he's given the assignment in New Orleans and everything changes. But will protecting Kate be something he can do without letting her in?

K.M. Scott writes contemporary romance stories of sexy, intense, and unforgettable love. A New York Times and USA Today bestselling author, she's been in love with romance since reading her first romance novel in junior high (she was a very curious girl!). Under her Gabrielle Bisset name, she write erotic paranormal and historical romance. She lives in Pennsylvania with a herd of animals and when she's not writing can be found reading or feeding her TV addiction.

Anina Collins has always loved a good mystery. From Agatha Christie's Hercule Poirot to Sir Arthur Conan Doyle's famous detective Sherlock Holmes to Dan Brown's intrepid Professor Robert Langdon, she's spent some of her favorite reading times with mystery novels. When she's not writing her favorite mystery couple, she can be found watching entirely too much Supernatural and dreaming about the beach.

Be sure to visit K.M.'s Facebook page at **facebook.com/kmscottauthor** for all the latest on her books, along with giveaways and other goodies! And to hear all the news on K.M. Scott books first, sign up for her newsletter today and be sure to visit her website at **www.kmscottbooks.com**

Visit Anina's Facebook page at **facebook.com/Anina-Collins-429334270597293** for news about her books, along with giveaways and other fun stuff! Sign up for her newsletter today for exclusive news first! Visit her website for more details at **aninacollins.com**

BOOKS BY K.M. SCOTT:

If I Dream (Corrupted Love #1)
If You Fight (Corrupted Love #2)
If We Fall (Corrupted Love #3)

Crash Into Me (Heart of Stone #1)
Fall Into Me (Heart of Stone #2)
Give In To Me (Heart of Stone #3)
Heart of Stone Volume One Box Set
Ever After (Heart of Stone #4)
A Heart of Stone Christmas (Heart of Stone #5)
Return To Me (Heart of Stone #6)
Forever With Me (Heart of Stone #7)
Heart of Stone Volume Two Box Set

Temptation (Club X #1)
Surrender (Club X #2)
Possession (Club X #3)
Satisfaction (Club X #4)
Acceptance (Club X #5)
The Complete Club X Series Box Set

Crave (Addicted To You #1)
Adore (Addicted To You #2)
Shatter (Addicted To You #3)
Claim (Addicted To You #4)
The Addicted To You Box Set

Hard Work (Standalone)

K.M.'S BOOKS ARE IN AUDIOBOOK TOO!

Books by K.M. Scott writing as Gabrielle Bisset:

Vampire Dreams Revamped (A Sons of Navarus Prequel)
Blood Avenged (Sons of Navarus #1)
Blood Betrayed (Sons of Navarus #2)
Longing (A Sons of Navarus Short Story)
Blood Spirit (Sons of Navarus #3)
The Deepest Cut (A Sons of Navarus Short Story)
Blood Prophecy (Sons of Navarus #4)
Blood Craving (Sons of Navarus #5)
Blood Eclipse (Sons of Navarus #6)
The Sons of Navarus Box Set #1
The Sons of Navarus Box Set #2

Stolen Destiny (Destined Ones Duology #1)
Destiny Redeemed (Destined Ones Duology #2)

Love's Master
Masquerade
The Victorian Erotic Romance Trilogy

Books by Anina Collins:

The Eleventh Hour (Poppy McGuire Mysteries #1)
After Hours (Poppy McGuire Mysteries #2)
Top of the Hour (Poppy McGuire Mysteries #3)
The Darkest Hour (Poppy McGuire Mysteries #4)
Happy Hour (Poppy McGuire Mysteries #5)
The Witching Hour (Poppy McGuire Mysteries #6)
The Finest Hour (Poppy McGuire Mysteries #7)